# MY NAME IS MILENA ROKVA

# MY NAME IS MILENA ROKVA

T.A. MACLAGAN

This is a work of fiction.
Any resemblance to persons living or dead is purely coincidental.

My Name Is Milena Rokva


Cover and Interior Design by Molly Phipps

ISBN: 9781983274091

First Edition

*To Mom, Dad, and Zac for being the most awesome family a girl could hope for!*

# PROLOGUE

*If you know the enemy and know yourself, you need not fear the result of a hundred battles. If you know yourself but not the enemy, for every victory gained you will also suffer a defeat. If you know neither the enemy nor yourself, you will succumb in every battle.*

Sun Tzu, *The Art of War*

## *Olissa - Two months before I became a cadet at Compound Perun and four years before I became Alexandra Gastone.*

I FELT FATHER'S gaze as I studied the chessboard. After an hour, our game was nearing an end, and for the first time, I saw a clear path to victory. Over the last year, my chess game had slowly improved. I could see four moves ahead instead of only one or two. I tried to contain my excitement, not wanting to alert Father to his impending doom. Neither my brothers nor I had ever beaten him. He wasn't the type of man to throw a game even for his children. What you won, you earned.

"Don't dawdle, Little O, or next game I'll add a timer and make it blitz chess. You're thinking too slowly."

"Zakhar," said Mom. "Milena's only seven. Play nice."

Father waved away her comment. "Fa. Chess is a brutal game, and you must be brutal to play it."

Mom flicked a well-aimed dishrag at him, catching him in the arm. Thwap. She shook her head with narrowed eyes. "Honestly, Zakhar. It's a game. The kids should learn sportsmanship, not brutality."

Father laughed and swatted her bottom. Normally Mom would have giggled, but instead, she shot him an angry look. Since his return, things between them had been unusually tense. My brothers and I had no idea why and were working hard to keep our heads down. "You understand don't you, Little O?" asked Father, winking. "You've got the killer instinct."

I nodded bashfully and moved my bishop diagonally three spaces putting the knight guarding Father's king into peril. In one more move, I would have him in check. My fingers twitched in anticipation. Our father was going down! My brothers would be so mad I was the first to beat him, and Mom would love giving him a hard time about losing. I couldn't wait. Maybe the mood in the house would finally lighten.

Father's face was impassive as he gazed at the board. He played fast, usually making a move within a few seconds, but this time, his fingers weren't flying to the board. Did he finally realize I had him? I stuffed my hands under my legs to stop my fingers from dancing and slumped back in my chair.

After maybe a minute, Father looked up, cocked his head to the side and grinned. "Do you realize where you went wrong, Little O?"

"What?" I squeaked, sitting up and darting my eyes over the board. I couldn't see anything that was off. My knight and rook guarded my king and … crap.

"You were so busy with your offense, you forgot about your defense. Check," said Father, replacing my rook with his own.

I balled my hands in frustration. I'd been so close. He'd beaten me to check by one lousy move. I narrowed my eyes and growled at the board, which only made him laugh. "See Sibel, I am teaching her about sportsmanship … Now, now, O. Play nice."

I glared at Father and moved my bishop in to protect my king and take him out of check.

On her way back through the dining room, Mom paused to give me a quick kiss on the cheek. "Don't let him get to you sweetheart. Your father can be an ass sometimes. Chess is just a silly game. Why don't you go outside and play?" A look passed between my parents like they were both ready to square off. Then Father cocked his head to the side and blinked, innocently. Mom's brow furrowed, and she threw her dishtowel on the chessboard with a harrumph.

I shrieked and hopped from my seat. "Mom, no."

I plucked up the towel, tossed it to her and immediately set to righting the toppled pieces. "Don't mess with the board. This is battle."

Mom studied me for a long moment until tears pricked her eyes and her lower lip quivered. She turned away to wipe at her cheeks and my stomach plummeted, twisting uncomfortably. I'd never seen Mom cry. Never. What was I supposed to do to help? Somehow I didn't think giving Mom a hug and kiss and telling her to go outside and play was going to do it. "I'm sorry Mom. I didn't mean to make you cry."

She patted my shoulder. "It's fine, sweetheart. Mommy's just a bit emotional today." Mom dabbed at her eyes with the dishtowel as she wandered into the kitchen. She made a point not to look at Father.

Because she wouldn't look at him, I did. He shrugged and rolled his eyes. "It's her angry time of the month," he whispered with a smile. I didn't smile back.

The chess pieces back in their rightful places, it was Father's turn, and he quickly moved his rook into position to steal my knight. I responded by moving my bishop in to block. I was not going down without a fight.

We continued to play for twenty more minutes, and despite my earlier setback, I was starting to feel that niggle of excitement again. I was nowhere near a checkmate, but I was also nowhere near losing. I had Father trapped in a stalemate. Studying the board, he emitted a barely audible grumble of which I doubted he was aware. I felt giddy. It wasn't a win, but it wasn't a loss. My brothers would still be green with envy.

When Father looked from the board to me, I grinned, waiting for his congratulations. Instead, he raised an eyebrow, his lips curling with distaste. "What are you so proud of?"

"I didn't lose," I said. Not wanting to shrink under the weight of his gaze, I kept my chin up and my eyes unblinking. There was something scary in his eyes, but I wasn't going to let him make me sad like Mom. I would be strong for the both of us. Still, my spine tingled as if I were prey.

Without warning, Father grabbed his queen and scattered the rest of the chess pieces with a swipe of his arm. "You play to win, or you don't play at all," he roared, flicking the queen toward me. It skidded across the board and fell into my lap.

Immobilized by shock, my pretense of strength evaporated. I quaked in my seat like a mouse facing down a voracious cat. I bowed my head, too nervous to look Father in the eyes. My twitching fingers fondled the ebony queen in my lap.

What had I been thinking? I flipped the queen over and rubbed a thumb across her pointed crown. She was the best piece and could move anywhere. She was powerful and Father's favorite strategic weapon. He used her with boldness and cunning. Of course, he wouldn't congratulate me on a stalemate. I should have known from how he played, unapologetically and always to win.

I flinched as the front door slammed, Father storming out. I didn't know whether to be relieved or terrified. Drawn by the commotion, Mom returned. I glanced up. Now I was the one fighting back tears. Mom's face was stricken as she rushed over. She picked me off the chair and sat down herself. Wrapping me in a hug, she rocked from side-to-side. "It's just a silly game, Milena, and sometimes your father's a silly man. If he's a poor sport, then refuse to play with him. Sometimes it takes more courage not to play." She kissed the top of my head. Once. Twice. Three times. "Your father's had a hard life. That's why he's sometimes like this. He still loves you."

We both jumped when the front door opened then slammed shut. Father was outside all of two minutes but had regained his composure. His face was quiet, neither mad nor sorry. It was like his outburst had never happened. He eyed us in the chair before marching over and taking a seat opposite. I shrunk further into Mom's arms. "Don't coddle her, Sibel. Little O, pick up the pieces. Let's play again."

Mom hugged me tighter. "Zakhar, no. There's been enough chess today. Milena, why don't you go outside and play with your brothers. Get some fresh air."

Father shot Mom a look then turned to me with another wink. “Come on, do battle one last time. Then we'll go out and find your brothers.” His voice was breezy, playful even. Had I only imagined his anger? This was the man I knew and loved. The man I wanted to make proud.

“Zak,” said Mom, her tone uncompromising. She smoothed a hand over my hair and kissed my cheek again. I'd been getting a lot of kisses lately. Far more than usual. I hugged her back thinking she must need the comfort because of her fight with Father.

Buried in the protective warmth of Mom's embrace, I peered across the table, studying my father. Although his outburst unsettled me, there was one thing I knew. I could beat him. I was getting closer every day. Maybe the next game would be *the one*.

Hungry for victory, I stood, wiped the embarrassing wetness from my cheeks and squared my shoulders. “It's okay Mom; I want a rematch.”

Father chuckled “There's my girl. Always game for another go.” He glanced at Mom with a smirk, and an *I told you so* look. Then his eyes fell to me. He smiled wide and winked. “My little soldier.”

# ONE

## *December 23rd - Two months after the gala*

"THERE SHE IS," said Albert, following Isra with his binoculars. "Just like clockwork."

I jotted down Isra's location and the time. Isra, a.k.a. Anna Kincaid, fiancée to up-and-coming Senator Michael Wilcox Jr., was my fellow Perun cadet. Albert and I were in our car outside the art gallery she co-owned with a friend, watching her on her usual three p.m. coffee break. Isra definitely had a routine, which made tailing her both extremely easy and extremely boring.

We'd been tailing Isra and Maxim, a.k.a. Perry Donovan—the head of City Energy New York, for more than a month now. After the CIA blew my cover as Alexandra Gastone, Albert, the *grandfather* I'd lived with for seven years, aided by his Agency friend, helped me escape my CIA captors. Now we were both fugitives. But instead of hiding in a cabin in the Yukon like smart fugitives, we were tailing the two Perun cadets I knew the locations for, in the hopes of uncovering points of contact with other cadets and handlers.

Basically, we were trying to untangle Perun's sleeper agent web looking for a juicy target. Someone that we could trade to the CIA for immunity. Albert was in his seventies, and I did not want him living the rest of his life on the lam. At the same time, I also didn't want to give up my fellow cadets. We needed someone high up the ladder, someone who'd been instrumental in orchestrating the taking and training of hundreds of children for use as long-term sleepers. I was personally hoping to nab Mistress, the vile woman who'd made my life at Compound Perun a living hell on more than one occasion. I would have no trouble trading Mistress for immunity. No trouble whatsoever!

Albert dropped the binoculars and shifted in his seat, running a hand up under his thigh. "My sciatica is killing me with all this surveillance, and don't get me started on my neck."

I laughed. "Tell me about it. My butt's growing exponentially each day." I made a twirling motion with my hand, "Turn around and I'll give you a quick neck massage." I moved to my knees and dug my thumbs into Albert's neck. "You're a rock. We should both be going to yoga classes like Isra."

"I'd stand out like a sore thumb," chortled Albert. "I've got forty years on all those kids."

I leaned into one of his knots and Albert groaned. "They'd eat you right up. You'd probably get two or three invitations for smoothies afterward."

"Only two or three? I must be losing my looks."

"Hah, hah," I said, doing a final karate chop across Albert's shoulders before turning to Orkney in the backseat and giving him a scratch behind the ears. Ork's giant form sprawled across the seat; his head propped on Albert's suitcase. I glanced at my watch. We needed to leave in half an hour if we wanted to get Albert to the airport on time.

In addition to surveillance, we'd spent our time as fugitives coming up with a plan to extract Albert's real granddaughter from Olissa. After I was captured, the CIA strong-armed me into attending the White House gala celebrating the newly elected Olissan President Vladik Kasarian. Chatter in the intelligence community suggested a hitter might be in play, and my captors wanted me on-site to identify any potential Perun cadets. Although I didn't end up recognizing any cadets and Perun resorted to using Kasarian's nut allergy in an attempt to off him, I did stumble upon someone I believed long dead—the real Alexandra Gastone.

After our switch, Perun must have discovered Alexandra was far smarter than the gathered intel suggested and decided to cultivate her as an asset. In a scenario very similar to my insertion, but with a helicopter crash replacing a car crash, Alexandra was inserted into the life of Vladik Kasarian, as his sister Alina. This all happened years before his Presidential run, of course. Perun was good at planning ahead. I identified Alexandra from the bell-shaped scar on her wrist, a scar we shared, and from the glass eye hiding the heterochromia we'd both been born with. After many heated debates and hours spent planning, Albert would leave for Olissa within hours, on a mission to free his real granddaughter.

Trying to ignore the pit in my stomach, I sank back in my seat. "You going to be alright continuing this surveillance without me?" asked Albert.

I mustered a smile. "I don't know. It's pretty challenging stuff. What with the sitting and watching … and watching some more. And of course, there's the whole needing to occasionally pee thing. What ever will I do?" I winked at Albert and leaned over to kiss his cheek. "Not to worry, old man. I've got this."

"I'm sorry about the timing Lex. I—"

"Albert," I growled.

He shook his head and grimaced. "Damn, Milena. I'm sorry. I'm trying. I really am, but I think you'll always be Lex to me."

"Try harder! You're about to liberate the real Alexandra. There can't be two Lexes in your life. It'll be confusing."

Albert nodded. "But you're okay with me going, right?" He appraised me with a wrinkled brow, his gaze running over the little black bird tattoo that now sliced through the bell-shaped scar on my wrist.

"I didn't tell you about Alexandra thinking you'd stay home and do nothing. I understand you need to go, and someone needs to stay here and keep up surveillance if we want that immunity deal."

"You're sure; you're fine?"

I patted his hand. "Quit worrying. It's all good. I am positively, almost certainly, probably not jealous of the real Alexandra Gastone. I want you to go and get her. We'll figure out everything else when you guys get back home." I gave Albert's hand a squeeze and then let go, taking up my binoculars and scanning the street. "I'm sure I'll fit into the mix somewhere. I'm not worried."

I'd left 'worried' behind long ago, trading it for perpetually terrified. What if Alexandra didn't want me in Albert's life? Sure, she'd been nice at the gala, but what if her feelings toward me had changed after she had time to digest my role in ruining her life? If I were in the same position, I wouldn't necessarily be thrilled with my imposter hanging around.

"You're my family. There will always be space for you."

"Yep. I know." I nodded to the street, grateful for the distraction. I didn't want to spend my last few hours with

Albert being touchy feely. I was holding it together pretty well and wanted to keep it that way. "Isra's coffee break is over." I jotted down the time. "She's living like a rebel and took an extra five minutes today."

Albert laughed, and we fell into a semi-comfortable silence for several minutes as Isra uncrated some paintings.

"Can you do me a favor?" Albert asked, when Isra disappeared into the backroom.

"You name it."

"Don't get any more tattoos while I'm gone, okay?"

Startled, I turned and found Albert stroking his eyebrows with worry. "What? Why?"

"It's a very emotional time for you with a lot of upheaval, and I don't want you doing anything you'll regret later." Albert tucked a lock of hair behind my ear. "Coloring your hair is one thing, but tattoos are different. I think one's enough."

I fingered my bangs. "I thought you liked the red."

"I do like the hair, it's … well … you've been making a lot of changes since the gala. I'm worried about you."

"Don't be. I'm fine." Unable to contend with Albert's worries when I had so many of my own, I returned my focus to Isra. *Nothing to look at here, Albert. Just the one tattoo and no others. Move along. Move along.*

ON THE WAY to the airport, Albert and I were able to recapture some of our original light-hearted banter. I'd vowed that Albert would go to Olissa feeling good about us. After all he'd done for me, he deserved to go and get his granddaughter without guilt or worry marring the reunion. "Tell me the plan for making contact again," I said.

Albert laughed. "You're a worry wart."

"You just spent the last ten minutes drilling me about my surveillance plans for Isra and Maxim. Turnabout is fair play. Humor me."

"Only if you promise not to approach Isra or Maxim yourself."

"Cross my heart, hope to die, stick a needle in my eye." I marked an X over my heart with a finger.

"Good! While you're keeping a safe distance from Perun operatives, I'm going to make contact with Brad's asset in Olissa who has arranged a janitorial position for me at the university where Alexandra lectures. From there I'll make contact."

"But not in person. Not the first time. Right?"

"I'll leave a written message for her after hours. I promise I won't make my first approach in person."

"I'm going to ask this one more time … you're absolutely, positively, without question, sure we can trust Brad? I know he helped me escape but ..."

"Yes, I'm sure. Brad is completely trustworthy. His asset is legit. I'm going to be perfectly safe."

"Fine. Just remember you're not a trained field op. You're a seventy-year-old analyst. You might not be able to spot her surveillance, and it will look weird if she's seen talking to the janitor. You need to be careful. If you love me, your first contact with Alexandra will not be in person."

"Of course I love you and ouch, bring my age into it why don't you." Albert laughed. "You're sweet to worry so."

"I'm serious Albert. You'd better not get caught, because if you do I'm coming over to save your ass, and we both know how much you want to keep me from having any fun."

"Language," said Albert, putting his hands up. "I got it. I'll be the poster boy for caution."

"Good," I said, elbowing him. "And make sure to check in with me every forty-eight hours."

"Yes, Mom."

"And tell me your new name again. You're always forgetting."

Albert's eyes rolled to the sky as he pretended to think. "Thomas Bennett?"

I slapped his arm. "Very amusing. It's Bennett Thompson. You need to respond when people call you that."

"Aye, aye, Lara Thompson," said Albert, throwing my new name, the one I hated, back at me. "I've got it."

"And be careful what you eat. Olissan food can be spicy, and you'll get heartburn."

Albert laughed long and loud. "We're a pair aren't we? Two nervous nellies."

"We're something all right." I pulled to the curb at La Guardia and hopped out to help Albert with his bags.

I lugged Albert's big suitcase out of the back while he stole his carry-on out from under Ork's head. "You take good care of her Orkney," said Albert.

Ork wuffed and licked Albert's hand. Albert kissed him on the snout, gave his face a good scratch then closed the back door. He set his suitcase on the curb and unzipped it, taking out two wrapped presents, one of which was definitely a dog bone. "These are for you and Ork. I'm sorry about missing Christmas."

I took the gifts and pulled Albert into a hug. "I've hidden something for you inside your big suitcase. Don't open it until Christmas, okay?"

Albert nodded, squeezing me tight. "You'll be okay by yourself for Christmas? I could get Brad—"

"I won't be alone. I've got a triple feature at the movies planned along with some Chinese take out for dinner. I'll be okay. I'm a big girl. No babysitter needed."

Albert hugged me closer, tucking his chin atop my shoulder. "We'll go to New Zealand next year," he said, referring to the Christmas trip he'd planned before the CIA blew my cover. "You, me and Alexandra. We'll all go."

I pulled away. "Sounds great," I said, my throat constricting as I battled back my emotions. Thankfully my voice didn't crack. *Keep it together, girl. Keep it together. Albert IS going to leave without guilt or worry.* I gestured to the cars lined up behind us, waiting for a spot. "I'd better get going."

"Are you sure I can't buy you dinner?" asked Albert, his eyebrows raised high and hopeful. "You can park, and I'll meet you inside?"

My throat still tight, I choked down a breath and shook my head. "Ork's gonna need a walk soon."

Ork had his nose pressed eagerly to the glass and Albert reached out a tentative hand, resting it on the window. A tear clung to Albert's eyelid and my stomach flip-flopped. We were doing an excellent job of holding it together. I brushed the tear away with my thumb then threw my arms around Albert again. I hadn't seen him cry since he found me in the hospital in Prague. "No tears, old man. No tears."

Albert sniffed. "Okay."

"Love you lots," I said, darting around to the driver's side door.

I caught Albert's "Love you, too" as I turned the key and peeled away.

# TWO

TWISTING MY KEY, I shoved at the safe house door with a hip as I scanned the street one last time. The brick row house apartments in this lower-middle-class Queens neighborhood were tidy, with tenants who worked hard during the day and minded their own business at night. At almost ten p.m., the lights were out in every apartment except for Mrs. Mulcahy's, the insomniac. Although the area lacked the country charm of Albert's Fair Valley farmhouse on the outskirts of D.C., our apartment was a perfect haven to hide in. My scan revealed nothing out of the ordinary. There were no new cars, and no one was walking an unknown dog.

With an annoyed wuffle, Ork nudged past me and walked into the hallway, heading for our door and his food bowl. I'd picked up Wendy's, and inside our tiny kitchen, Ork attached himself to my hip, until I pulled out his two cheeseburgers, tore them up and deposited them in his bowl. "Don't tell Albert. He'll get mad," I said, mussing the wiry fur on his head. With Ork attacking his meal, I plopped my cheeseburger and fries on a plate, grabbed my Frosty, and headed into the den for some much-deserved TV time.

Albert always made us sit at the kitchen table to eat. "We might be fugitives, but we're not barbarians," he'd say. But now that he was off to Olissa, I figured what the hell. There ought to be some perks to flying solo.

I flicked through the channels looking for something to get lost in. We only had ten channels, so that didn't take long. Most everything was on a commercial, so I was on my third pass before I stumbled on the beginning of *Love Actually*. If anything could distract me from Albert's absence, it was fatty food and Andrew Lincoln with a large side helping of Hugh Grant and Colin Firth.

After finishing his dinner, Ork hopped up next to me and eyed what remained of my burger. I nudged him with my elbow. "Forget it, buddy. This is my comfort food. You've had yours." Ork popped up an eyebrow and sighed mournfully. "I know you miss him too, but we're going to be fine. We've got lots of work to do. Isra needs contacting and potentially extracting. Maxim needs watching. We'll hardly notice Albert's gone." Ork arched his opposite brow and ruffed. "He bought you a big bone for Christmas. Do you want it?" I asked, falling prey to Ork's too cute, seesaw eyebrows.

Not trusting Ork, I gathered up my food and went to retrieve his bribe. "Yum, yum," I said, returning and presenting him with the bone-shaped package. I peeled the wrapping paper slowly to build his anticipation. I couldn't help but smile when Ork licked his chops. He snatched the bone when it was three-fourths revealed and pawed away the rest of the paper himself. Score one for Albert in the Christmas gift department.

I'd grabbed my present as well and now eyed it. Albert and I traveled almost every Christmas, so we kept our gifts simple. Just one or two presents a piece. I'd had to think long and hard about what to get this year given our fugitive status and all that happened. How do you say, "thank you for rescuing me from the clutches of the CIA when I'm not even your real granddaughter?" I'd eventually blown the budget and spent three hundred bucks on an 1839 edition of Nicholas Nickleby, one of Albert's favorite Dickens novels. The book was an unnecessary extravagance, but I didn't know what was going to happen when Albert brought Alexandra home and wanted him to have something special. Given our book club tradition, I figured a book was the perfect gift.

Deciding Albert would never know if I opened my present early and curious as to what he'd gotten me, I grabbed the gift and started to peel the paper at the edges. I worked slowly, wanting to savor the moment. From the shape, it looked like Albert had also gone the book route. I crossed my fingers for a good fantasy, something that would whisk me away and get me through the holidays. Once the end of the package was open, I peeked inside. Yep, I was right—a book. My skills of deduction were still in top form. Go me.

The book was leather with gold embossing at the paper's edge, definitely not your typical bookstore hardcover. "Albert, you better not have gotten me an 1839 edition of Nicholas Nickleby," I muttered, tearing away the rest of the paper. I'd opened the package to the back cover and quickly flipped it over to see the title. "Really?" I said, opening the cover to read Albert's note.

*Sometimes writing your story down is the first step toward getting past it.*

*Love, Grandpa*

First, a gun for my birthday and now a journal, because that was on every spy's wish list. We loved to write down our secrets so anyone could find them. And *getting past what?* I was all right. I had it together. Mostly.

I was busy glaring at the journal when my phone rang. I dived for it, knowing it was Martine because the only other person who might call was somewhere over the Atlantic. In addition to me discovering the real Alexandra Gastone at Vladik Kasarian's gala, my best friend Martine, accompanying her diplomat father (D.C. is a surprisingly small world), saw through my disguise because of the unique tattoo on my back. Needless to say, she surmised something weird was up, and after the gala she relentlessly barraged my phone and email with questions. Albert and I talked and agreed I could reveal the truth if Brad ran a background check and it came back clean, which of course it did.

I checked the incoming number to make sure it came from the burner phone I'd sent. 555-1686. Martine was following protocol. I sank back into the couch with a smile and clicked the green answer button. "How's my favorite friend?"

"Aren't I your only friend?"

"Details. Details," I said with a laugh. "So how are you?"

"I'm good. Just wanted to check in. Albert's going out-of-town soon right? You'll be alone?"

And this was why Albert agreed to tell Martine the truth. He wanted someone else to keep tabs on me while he was away. Martine was perfect for the job. "Albert grabbed a train this morning, and I'm not alone. I've got Ork. He's great company." Although I trusted Martine with my secret, I wasn't willing to tell her anything specific about what Albert and I were up to. She could know he was gone but not where he was going or how he was getting there.

"Well, as long as you won't be lonely."

"I won't," I replied, trying to sound neither defensive nor suspiciously chipper.

Several long heartbeats of silence followed before Martine broke the uncomfortably dead air with a very loud, "Guess who I ran into at the mall today?"

My stomach did a somersault. There was only one person we both knew, who she'd bother to mention. Grant. "How is he?" I asked, sucking in a nervous breath.

"Good. He asked about you. Apparently, he's been checking with some of the rehab places in D.C. and Virginia to find out where you are so he can visit. He figures rehab must have friends and family days, and he wants to be a good boyfriend. He's worried about you. I know you said he was a sweetheart, but that's going above and beyond."

I wiggled uncomfortably in my seat. I'd thought rehab was a good excuse for my absence. I'd thought he'd get on with his life, but instead, he was still doing the awesome boyfriend thing.

"Do you think you should ..." Martine trailed off, her words hanging heavy in the void between us.

"Break up with him?" The words felt weighty in my mouth. If I wanted to do right by Grant, I needed to let him go.

"I was going to suggest telling him the truth."

"I don't think that's a good idea." I nudged Ork's bone with my toe. Annoyed, Ork pushed my foot away with his cold, wet nose.

"Why not? You told me."

"You already knew something was up. You saw me in disguise at a Presidential function."

"You love him, right?"

"Yes, but—"

"But nothing. He deserves to know."

"I'm a wanted criminal, and his father works for the Agency. His dad's the one who captured me."

"You and Albert are working to bring down Perun and

get immunity, right? Maybe one day you won't be fugitives. Criminals get immunity all the time when they help catch bad guys."

"It's not that simple—"

"Well, it could be, couldn't it? I think you should lay out the situation. That you're a badass spy, and you love him, and you can't be with him right now, but you're doing your damnedest to get immunity so maybe someday you could. Then he can decide for himself. You've left him in limbo without all the facts, which is cruel. He's not moving on."

I fell silent as my mind picked at Martine's logic. Martine hardly batted an eye when I'd told her the truth, but she wasn't exactly normal. She'd thought it was cool. Moviesque even. The games nations played with each other, and my part in them, didn't matter to her. She'd said she knew me at my core—that I loved Orkney, Albert, and dance—and that's what mattered. Would Grant see things the same way? I had my doubts. And then there was the issue of his dad. If he got even a hint Grant was in contact with me; I'd be putting myself at greater risk and Grant in a terrible position. Staying in the States to go after Perun and an immunity deal was already risky enough. "Grant will hate me for all the lies. He'll never understand."

"He definitely won't if you don't give him a chance. He loves you. What about his poem on the back of that photo? The *eyes spy loss, I spy danger* one. Doesn't he already know you?"

I looked at Ork happily gnawing his bone. Did Grant really know me? When I saw his words on that picture, I'd thought he did. I thought he saw deep into my soul. Was there a chance he could get past all the lies if I took a leap and told him the truth? Should I take the risk? If I broke up with him, he'd be lost to me. If I told him the truth, he might run, but then again he might not.

But what if his father had already told him about me, and Grant was using Martine to bait a trap? Grant wasn't a good actor, though. He was almost laughably bad. If I surprised him with a visit, his bad acting and nerves would reveal if he already knew about me. If not, his true feelings about my past as a spy, for better or worse, would come to light. The only chance for us to make it was to tell him the truth. I had nothing to lose except everything.

"Don't be wimpy," said Martine, breaking the silence.

"You're right," I said. "I'll tell him."

Martine squealed. "Yes! I just know he's going to understand. Call me after and tell me everything. He mentioned his dad was going to be working Christmas Eve, so maybe you could go tomorrow. You could have the whole day together. Wouldn't that make for a happy holiday?"

"We'll see. It's a six-hour drive. I might go tomorrow if the roads are clear," I said, my stomach threatening to regurgitate a partially digested cheeseburger. I might not have much to lose, but that didn't mean the thought of spilling the beans to Grant wasn't nerve-wracking.

AFTER TALKING TO Martine, I bailed on *Love Actually* and dinner for a hot shower, hoping it would relax my nerves. I'd kept my secrets bottled up for so many years; I wasn't used to the idea of giving them away. As hard as keeping secrets was, the thought of sharing them seemed harder somehow.

Shedding my clothes, I looked at my reflection in the mirror, trying to envision what Grant would see—once he got beyond ogling my girl parts, because … well ... boys are boys. Would he like the changes? The red hair? The tattoos? Was it all too much for the poster boy of wholesome? I twisted slowly in the mirror to see my first tattoo, the black and white swans between my shoulder blades. My Odette and Odile. They had been the two sides of my life as Alexandra Gastone, the spy I was and the high school girl I pretended to be. I wasn't Lex Gastone anymore, though. I was finally Milena Rokva. Too bad I had no idea who Milena was or wanted to be.

I shifted to study my more recent additions, a flock of birds flying free from their broken cage at the curve of my hip. There were twelve little black birds now, eleven scattering to my stomach and back, the last bird on my wrist, slicing through my scar. Each bird was unique. Each was a different visit to the tattoo shop. Each was an effort at staying sane.

Running a finger from one little bird to the next, I wondered if my tattoos would be too much for Grant if we ever found ourselves … without clothes. Would the tattoos intrigue Grant or repulse him?

I loved Grant. I was nothing like him, but I loved him. I was attracted to my opposite, but would he be attracted to his? He'd loved wholesome, girl next door, Alexandra Gastone, and I was neither wholesome nor the girl next door. I hadn't realized how stifling I'd found that persona until I was able to shed it. Even if he could forgive the spy thing, I wasn't sure Grant could love who I really was. But I had to take the chance right? Big risks, yield big rewards or so the motivational posters say.

Using the tips of my finger, I pulled out my brown contacts and deposited them in their solution then gazed into my real eyes. "You are Milena Rokva," I whispered. "Not Lara Thompson and definitely not Alexandra Gastone. You are Milena. You must remember."

Without realizing it, I found myself pointing at the mirror. "Don't forget. Even if Grant wants Alexandra, you can only be you. From now on, you are only Milena Rokva, whoever the hell she is."

# THREE

UNABLE TO SLEEP, I hit the road around midnight and arrived on the outskirts of Fair Valley before sunrise. Mark, Grant's dad, wouldn't leave for work for several hours, so I found a highway dive I was sure none of my Fair Valley friends or acquaintances would ever visit and parked my butt to wait along with Ork. The waitress gave Ork a wary glance. "He's a service dog," I said, offering my most winning smile. "I have diabetes."

She eyed Ork for several seconds, then shrugged. The diner had one patron … me, and I doubted health inspectors made their rounds before the sun was up. Not wanting to arrive at Grant's with a fuzzy mind and bleary eyes, I ordered a large coffee and a side of toast then added a rare steak when Ork cocked his head to the side and looked at me sweetly. My stomach hadn't stopped its rollercoaster ride since I'd made the decision to tell Grant the truth. I could stare down the barrel of a gun and not flinch, or face a man twice my size in hand-to-hand combat without a second thought, but ask me to visit the boy I loved and lied to for over a year, and I was sweating bullets. Go figure. I felt resolved, though.

Good result or bad, this needed to be done. With his calls to local rehab centers searching for me, Grant wasn't letting the relationship go and on my end, if Albert and I managed to nab an immunity deal, I would love to think Grant might be a part of my future. Both of us deserved to know if there was even the remotest possibility of a future us. We needed to open the door to our future or close it forever. Anything less was just unhealthy.

I headed over to Grant's after twiddling my thumbs for an hour and a half and downing way too many cups of coffee. I was so caffeinated; I practically vibrated. As luck would have it, Mark's car pulled out of the garage as I arrived. In less than half an hour, he would be installed behind his desk at Langley and part of his day might consist of gathering intel on my whereabouts. If I wasn't so nervous, I might have laughed. After catching me in a trap, zapping me with a taser, and threatening jail if I didn't help the CIA, Mark wasn't exactly my favorite person.

I drove past the house and circled the street looking for any surveillance. Albert's SUV had tinted windows, so I wasn't worried about being spotted if someone was watching the house. Once I got out of the car, however, that would be a different story, so I popped on my winter hat and grabbed a scarf. Coupled with my wide-rimmed sunglasses, the props covered most of my face. The combo was as good at hiding my identity as a ski mask and a whole lot less suspicious. Winter, with all its bulky clothes and wraps, was a great season for walking around unidentifiable.

I parked down the street and slipped out of the car, leaving Ork to his morning post-meal siesta. My eyes swiveled back and forth between the front door and my surroundings as I walked. Spying 101 called for me to focus solely on my broader environment as I was in a danger zone, but the damn door kept pulling my focus. "Should I ring the bell or let myself in like always?" I muttered to myself. I approached, slowly, doing one last appraisal of my surroundings. Finding them clear, I reached for the doorknob then stopped, my fingers twitching. Was this the right call? Or was it too informal for having been gone so long? Quick as lightning, I skirted my hand over to the doorbell and slammed it down before I could change my mind. There. Decision made.

When no one came to the door after fifteen very long seconds, I rang the bell again and looked back over my shoulder, darting my eyes to the left and right. Another fifteen seconds passed. It was seven in the morning, and Grant was always up by six—it didn't matter if he was sick, it was school holidays, or he'd been out late partying—he was hardwired. He should be up, damn it.

*Screw it.* I tried the door handle, and as it squeaked open, I caught the telltale sound of Radiohead coming from upstairs. Yep, he was up. I took the stairs two at a time, not wanting time to talk myself out of anything, my focus and intent like a linebacker bearing down on the quarterback for a sack. I gulped a quick breath outside his bedroom door and then knocked.

There was lots of rustling and then the door popped open. "You forget something … Oh my God …"

I inhaled sharply. Grant was wearing jeans and a nice set of abs. Yes, he was still gangly, but he was my kind of gangly. My heart fluttered, and my stomach did a loop-dee-loop. Grant's eyes went wide behind his glasses and then his dimples appeared along with a gargantuan smile. Before I could say anything, he grabbed me in a giant hug and swung me around. After a big, happy kiss, he set me down then stepped back to look me over. "You look fantastic. Healthy." He grabbed me in a hug again. "It's so good to see you, Lex.

God, I've missed you." He started swinging me in circles as he walked across the room. Then, in typical Grant fashion, he tripped over his gym shoes, and we pitched onto his bed.

"Shit," said Grant, pulling back. "You okay? Sorry."

Truly happy for the first time in days, I could only laugh as I rolled on top of him. "I'm great," I said, leaning down to give him a proper kiss. "I love you so ..."

The words escaped before I consciously realized what I was saying. What was I doing? I hadn't come for this. It wasn't fair to say such things before coming clean.

Seemingly oblivious to the words catching in my mouth, Grant smiled. "You don't know how long I've been waiting for you to say that in-person and not over the phone. I love you, too."

Not knowing what to do, I returned his smile as we locked eyes. I wanted to look away but couldn't. This was going all wrong, but it felt so right. I reached out and ran my fingertips over the arch of one cheekbone. God, he was so beautiful. So normal. So beautifully normal.

Grant tucked a stray piece of hair behind my ear. "Red, huh? I like it."

"It's the new me." I ran a tentative hand through my hair. "You really like it? I think Albert hates it."

Grant's brows furrowed. "Albert? You mean your grandpa?"

I stifled a grimace. Note to self: remember who you're talking to. "Yes, of course, my grandfather. Back to the hair. You like it?"

"It's different. Edgy. But yeah, I like it," he replied, tickling my nose with a piece.

I smiled, presenting my wrist. "I got a tattoo!" If he liked the hair, then maybe …

Grant grabbed my hand. "Holy shit. No way. Dude, you've

gone all badass ..." Grant's words trailed off. For a brief second, he'd been excited, then poof, it evaporated, his face going blank. "How did you get a tattoo in rehab?"

I did a mental head bonk. Could I screw things up any more? Grant tensed under me, probably to guard himself against another onslaught of lies.

And another lie is exactly what I gave him. "I'm on furlough for the holidays," I said, the words falling from my lips with ease. In a classic distract and evade move, I bumped my nose against Grant's, then leaned in for a kiss. I would kiss him, gather my thoughts, then tell him everything. I just needed a second.

I tried to pour my original sense of excitement at seeing Grant into the kiss but was coming up short. It didn't help that Grant was also holding back. After a few long seconds of second-rate kissing, I pulled away and rolled onto my back with a groan. Mirroring me, Grant did the same only with a tired sigh.

"Did you run away from rehab?" he asked.

"No."

"And that's the truth?"

Propping myself on an elbow, I peered down at Grant. "I am absolutely, 100 percent, telling you the truth. I didn't skip out on rehab." *You can't skip out on a place you've never been.*

"Then tell me how it was? You don't have to go into detail. Just give me something."

I nodded. "First, tell me what's been going on with you and the gang? Then I'll tell you everything." *Probably. If I can find the words and the courage. God, what are you going to think of me?*

Grant relaxed a little bit and smiled. "Football season ended good, not great. We made it to the regional playoffs. I'm going to Rutgers in the fall. I doubt I'll play much the first year, but I can see myself being really happy there. They have an excellent pre-law program, and it's not far from Princeton. We'd be able to see each other on the weekends if … well … if you want to."

I squeezed his hand. "You should take some photography classes too," I said, gesturing to the wall with his photo collages. He'd added another pattern since I'd seen it last, a sunflower, made up of macro shots. "Your pictures are beautiful." I found his eyes. "I mean that. Really beautiful. It'd be a shame not to do something with your talent." Maybe I was wrong, but I didn't think Grant had the heart of a lawyer.

Grant glanced at the eclipse pattern on his wall and blushed. The eclipse consisted of photos of me, myself and I and wasn't meant for my eyes. It laid Grant, the artist, bare and showed his frustration with our relationship and the walls I'd erected to protect myself. After spending the night in Grant's room before the gala, I'd left everything as I found it, except for opening my birthday present. Grant knew I'd been in his room, and that I'd seen his photos.

"Before I left for rehab, I came by to say goodbye. Your dad let me in so I could write a note." I leaned in and kissed Grant's cheek. "Thank you for the birthday present. It was perfect."

Grant flicked his eyes to the eclipse then back to me. "I—"

"You don't need to say anything. I know I wasn't the best girlfriend. I was distant, and I wouldn't let you in. But I want to tell you the truth, about rehab, about all of it. I just hope you'll be able to forgive me. I hope that maybe we can move forward because I really do love you."

Grant peeled himself off his pillow and took my hand in his, his fingers absently finding the bell-shaped scar, just like always. His lips brushed mine for the briefest of kisses. Warm and sweet. Mint and oranges. *Everything will be fine,* they seemed to say.

I tried to lose myself in that brief moment. But I couldn't.

"Lex, whatever you have to say, I love you. No matter what. We'll be able to start again and be better … stronger than now."

Grant's words echoed as I tried to form my thoughts into something coherent. Catching sight of the eclipse behind Grant, I got up and scanned the images, running my hand over the wall, until I found the one I was looking for. It was Martine's photo of me from the dance. Grant had modified it so that my eyes, one blue and one gray/green, stood out above all else. I turned the photo over and handed it to him.

I knew the words on the back all too well. I'd replayed them hundreds of times. A day hadn't passed that I didn't visualize Grant's handwriting and his words. Sometimes in my sleep, he spoke them to me.

I spy beauty
Eyes spy loss
I spy strength
Eyes spy death
I spy knowledge
Eyes spy danger
I spy potential
Eyes spy distance

"I spy a lie?" I said, finding Grant's eyes.

Grant's face went ashen, and I touched his cheek. "You're not wrong. What I'm about to tell you, you can't tell anyone. Ever." I looked him hard in the eyes.

Grant laughed. "Dramatic much?"

"I mean it."

Grant raised his hands in surrender. "Sure. I won't tell anyone. I promise." Grant gestured for me to sit, but I knelt in front of him instead. I needed to face him … this … head on.

"What I'm about to tell you will seem crazy. But I swear it's all true."

"Okay."

I gazed into Grant's eyes trying to find where to start. Finally, I took the photo from his hands. "You wrote *I spy a lie*, and you're not wrong. There has been so many." My throat tightened as I took Grant's hands in mine and kissed them. *Please, please, please don't hate me. Please.* "I'm not going to Princeton in the fall," I blurted, starting with a random bit of the truth for no apparent reason other than it seemed the easiest to say.

Grant's face fell, and he tried to say something, probably heartfelt words of support, but I cut him off with more truths. Truths poured out of me in a jumbled randomness. "I don't have a drug problem, and I call him Albert because he's not my real grandfather. I used to be a ballet dancer, and I never went to rehab. My parents didn't die in a car accident. My mom was murdered, but I think my dad is still alive. He's the one who gave me away to a place called Perun. My name's not Alexandra Gastone. I'm Milena Rokva, but Perun took that from me. They took my family and ballet. They took it all and gave me someone else's life. I'm from Olissa. I'm an Olissan spy."

Grant looked at me blank-faced. For one heartbeat. Two. Five. Ten.

"When you were at U Penn doing a campus visit, your dad was the one who caught me and forced me into a deal with the CIA." I babbled, not comfortable with the silence.

Grant reached out and swiped at a few escaped tears. His

touch wasn't gentle. "Quit messing around, Lex. That's not funny. Not funny at all." Before I could process what he'd said, Grant stood and pushed past me. "Jesus, Lex. Why can't you take our relationship seriously? I mean, shit." Grant waved his hands wildly "Ha ha. You're a spy," he said, his anger boiling, his voice rising to a yell.

I scrambled to my feet, my mind reeling. I'd been prepared for anger and maybe tears. But not disbelief. After seeing through so many of my lies, how could he not see my truth?

# FOUR

I WIPED AT my eyes with a sleeve trying to compose myself. "I didn't ask to be a spy. Not at first. I was a kid. My mom was murdered, and Perun used that. They made me want to avenge her death," I said, hoping he would somehow hear the sincerity in my voice. What had I been thinking? Of course, he wouldn't believe me. A teenage sleeper agent, cheerleader spy, it sounded like a popcorn movie for teens. Martine believed me only because she saw me in action at the gala. "I only wanted to help my people. Olissa has never been safe. Never. I'm so sorry for lying to you. I never wanted to. I love you. Please try to understand the position I was in."

Grant glanced at his words on the photo, then crumpled it. "Just leave. I'm done. With you. With this. It's not worth it. You're a liar and need help, but I can't deal with this anymore." He pointed to the door.

When I didn't immediately move, he went over and opened it. "Out!" he yelled, vibrating with hurt and barely contained rage. By telling him a truth he couldn't believe, I was tearing his heart in two. Our bond was shattering.

I stared unable to move. I tried to take a step, but my boots were lead. I couldn't let him ignore the truth. Having finally spoken it, having opened myself up in that way, I needed for him to at least believe me. Even if he still hated me, at least it would be for the right reason and not because he thought I was a pathological liar.

Latching onto an idea, I found my feet, and I was across the room a second later. I swept Grant's legs out from under him before he realized my intention. If he wouldn't believe my words, perhaps my combat skills could persuade him. I pinned Grant to the floor, his arms behind his back, then pulled the knife from my ankle holster. I put it to his throat so he could feel the edge of the blade. "I'm not lying," I said, my whole being screaming for him to believe me.

*Believe. Please, believe me.*

Furious, Grant struggled to break free. I let the pressure off his arms and stood, letting my knife drop to the floor. Grant scrambled up, grabbing the blade. He pointed it at me. "Jeez—"

I grabbed his hand with both of mine and twisted, applying pressure with my thumbs. The knife clattered to the ground. "I'm not lying."

*Believe. Believe. Believe.*

With lips curled in disgust, Grant grabbed both of my arms and shoved me backward. I hit the wall and for a second Grant's face was startled as if he couldn't believe he'd pushed me. Couldn't believe his fingers were digging into my arms like a vice. He glowered at me, his hands tightening even more as his gaze sank into me, ripping at my insides like a feral dog. He started shaking me. At first, it was a jiggle as his body fought the tension he held, but then it was an earthquake of hard fury. "Get out!"

I stomped down on his foot and then turned sideways, breaking his grip on my arms. I pushed him backward then landed a kick to his chest that sent him to the ground. I snagged the knife off the floor and was sitting on his chest a millisecond later.

*Believe.*

I peered down at Grant, but his eyes refused to find me now, instead darting every which way. His panic, the chaos of our fight, was keeping Grant from understanding. I grabbed his face and turned it to the wall of photographs. Grant growled like a rabid dog and jerked out of my grip. I grabbed him again, slamming his cheek into the floor. "I'm not lying," I said, throwing the knife.

Time seemed to slow as light from the window caught the silver blade somersaulting through the air. Mesmerized, Grant watched the blade's rotation as it headed for one of the photo collages on his wall—the eclipse made up of my photos. It buried itself where the darkness met the light. He gasped.

*Believe.*

I scrambled off Grant's chest and sank to the floor beside him. His eyes were still on the knife, but his panic was gone. In its place … understanding.

"I love you," I whispered.

"You're not lying?"

I grabbed his hand, grasping at forgiveness. "I'm not lying."

My heart beat so fast and loud; I could barely hear. My nerves hummed. My stomach churned. He believed me, but I didn't know what that meant. Not yet. How was this going to end? My whole body shook as I waited for an answer. Would what we shared be enough to overcome something so big?

Grant jerked his hand away and edged backward. He grabbed a shirt off his desk chair and shrugged it on as if it were armor and offered him some protection from my words, from the truth.

"I love you," I said again. I worked hard to make my voice stronger, more confident. I wanted him to know I wasn't lying. Not about my feelings for him.

"What part of us was true?" asked Grant, wedging his body between the bed and desk.

"The 'I love you' part," I offered, searching my memories. "The kisses were true. The handholding. The walks in the woods … Our plans to photograph the stars. Those parts were all true."

"That's all?" said Grant. "That's nothing. I don't know who you are."

His words carved at my insides. Those parts weren't nothing. They were everything. Near me was the crumpled photo. I grabbed it and peeled the edges back to flatten it. "You saw the real me," I said, turning it over and silently reading through his poem. "You saw all the bits of me I was keeping hidden. You spied the loss, the death, the danger. You saw it even though I never told you." I put the photo on the ground and pushed it toward him. "You saw it all. You may not know all the facts about me, but you know me deep down. You do."

Grant snatched the photo and studied his words then turned it over to look at my eyes. My curse. I sat silently. Waiting. Hoping for a miracle. Seconds ticked by. Minutes. Good God, what was he thinking? I searched his face for hints. Was that flicker behind his eyes anger? That tug on his lips, forgiveness? My mind writhed in purgatory wanting to know if this was a beginning or an end.

Finally, Grant turned his attention from the photo. He scanned me up, down and back again. I sat as still as a stone. Finally, his eyes locked with mine and held, all that we were, stretching before us. Would there be hope or was our future a void? I heard something crumpling but didn't look. I couldn't. What would it be? Forgiveness or the death of us?

At first, I could read nothing on Grant's face, but then came the shift. The veil fell. And what remained was … hatred. "Get out," he said, turning away. "Get the fuck out of my room."

# FIVE

## *January 15th*

I SMILED AT Albert's pixilated image on the computer screen. "Hi, Albert!"

"Hi Lex. How are you?" Albert leaned forward trying to see past me. "Where are you? It doesn't look like the safe house."

I crossed my arms and glared at the screen. How many times would I have to remind him? I'd been patient. I needed one thing from Albert, and one thing only, to get my name right.

"Can you hear me?" he asked, fiddling with his computer. "Am I on mute? Damn technology." Albert tapped on a bunch of different keys. "Can you hear me now?"

I cleared my throat. "My. Name. Is. Milena. Or M."

Albert looked up from his keyboard with an apologetic grimace and sat back, running a hand through his full head of gray. "I'm sorry Milena. Really I am. I'm not trying to get it wrong."

Perfect. Now I felt bad for being snarky. I knew he was

trying. We were both trying. "What's up with you?" I asked, glancing at my watch. "I can't talk super long today."

"How is surveillance of Isra and Maxim?"

"Fine. But I think it's time to reach out to Isra and let her know what's going on. We've been watching her for months now and have nothing to show for it. If we approach her directly, she might be able to give us some valuable intel on her points of contact within Perun. Isra was one of my closest friends, I know—"

"No. No. No," said Albert, whipping his head back and forth. "You promised you wouldn't. It's too dangerous."

"I laugh in the face of danger," I said, with a mischievous grin.

Albert bristled. "That's what I'm afraid of."

I rolled my eyes. "Jeez. I was joking. You used to laugh at my jokes."

"Humor doesn't translate well over the internet. So you won't approach them?"

I raised my arms in surrender. "Fine. I don't want you to worry. I won't mention it again." *I'll just do it instead.*

"I know you're probably getting lonely and tired of solo surveillance, so I have reinforcements coming your way. The agency owes Brad vacation time, so he's going to help you. He'll be at the safe house sometime today."

My jaw dropped. "I'm not lonely," I said, my voice squeaky and defensive.

Okay, being alone was a bit of a drag, and I had thought of bringing in my old handler, Varos. But I'd decided against it. Although Varos was the one to tell me about the fissure in Perun and their plan to control the world energy markets, I could still see his crazed eyes at our last meeting. He'd drawn a gun-shaped hand to my forehead and pulled a pretend trigger. His fingers dug in with each bang. Bang. Bang.

He'd been describing the execution of his parents, two loyal Perun collaborators. Something in Varos had snapped, and I didn't know if he could come back from it. He wasn't worth the risk.

Flying solo wasn't that bad. Albert was doing this because of the breakup with Grant. I should never have told him. I did not need nor want a babysitter. Sure I'd curled up in a ball for a couple of days post-breakup, and sure I'd eaten one too many pints of ice cream, but that was normal teenage girl stuff after getting dumped. I was fine now. Totally fine. Better than fine, in fact. I was great.

"It couldn't hurt to have the extra set of eyes. Besides, Brad doesn't do well with down time. You'll be doing him a favor."

"I'm not in the business of favors, Albert."

"He helped me rescue you," said Albert, staring me down across the internet ether.

I narrowed my eyes and grumbled, but that only made him smile, his blue eyes twinkling. "Fine," I finally said, shaking my head in disgust. Albert could always get to me with that smile. Jeez, Ork had his eyebrows, and Albert had his smile; I was such a sucker.

Albert chuckled. "Now that's settled, tell me why you aren't at the safe house."

"The furnace is busted. Ork is staying with Mrs. Mulcahy until it's fixed, but I wanted my privacy. Someone is coming to fix it tomorrow. How are things with Alexandra?" I asked, wanting to get Albert off the subject of the hotel.

"I left a message embedded in her research files detailing the extraction plan. I wanted to do a Wind-up Willy grab while she was leaving work, but she suggested extraction at the alternative energy conference she's attending in a few weeks. It's in Turkey, so that eliminates all the issues of trying to sneak her out of Olissa, where her *brother* is President.

Turkey will be much easier."

"Sounds like a—" I heard a tapping at my door.

"Housekeeping."

"Just a minute," I called. I smiled at Albert. "Housekeeping's here. Gotta go. Take care of yourself." I blew him a kiss and moved a finger to the disconnect button.

"Wait," called Albert. "Can you tell them to come back? I have something to tell you before Brad shows up."

The knock from housekeeping came again, and my heart revved. "Brad and I will be fine. Talk soon and say hi to Alin ... Alexandra for me."

I closed down Skype without waiting for Albert's reply. "Coming," I called. I paused for a second, smoothing my hair and gathering myself. I was ridiculously nervous and could barely stand still. My body wanted to run laps around the room. After sucking in a final steadying breath, I opened the door.

At seeing me, a broad, happy smile crossed the housekeeper's face, brightening her soulful gray eyes. It was a smile I knew well—a smile just like my mother's.

# SIX

"BACK SO SOON, Lara? Third time this month, yes?" asked the housekeeper.

"Hi, Amalya! Nice to see you. Yep, back again. You been up to much?" I smiled, studying her. I wanted to remember everything from the fine lines around her eyes to the color of her lipstick. Months before, when Albert revealed he knew I was a spy and had always known, he gave me a folder containing all the information he had on my family. It included a picture of Amalya, in her maid's uniform at this very hotel. It was your standard, poorly lit, ID photo and didn't do her justice. Despite years of hardship—my mother's death, my brothers' incarceration and going from prominent ballet teacher in Olissa to hotel maid in New York—my grandmother was still a beautiful woman. Regal. Her frame was strong from years of dance. The only thing hinting at all she'd gone through were her eyes. Although still bright, there was also an edge of wariness there. But like all Olissans, she was a survivor. I ached to hug her as I fingered the ballet tickets in my back pocket. Martine and I were going that night, and I'd purchased an extra one for

Amalya. Now, I needed to work up the nerve to ask her.

"Just work and book clubs!" She wheeled her cart toward the bed. "How are you?"

"I checked out that book you recommended. The one on finding your best self."

"You like?"

"Yeah, I did. I kinda need some help in that department. Finding the real me … the best me. So, it gave me a lot to think about."

Amalya laughed. "I think we all need help in that department. Is blonde hair part of finding better self?"

"Maybe," I said, smiling. "What do you think? Is it better than the red?"

She paused to study me. "You are pretty girl. I think all hair color is good. Blonde is nice. More natural than red." Amalya patted her head. "You think I should dye mine? I heard dyeing gray makes you look ten years younger."

"No way." Amalya's hair wasn't gray but a pure white. "Your hair is beautiful. Don't change a thing. If I'm lucky enough to get old, I'm going to wear my gray hair with pride."

Amalya shook her head. "Lucky enough? You have good genes. You will be fine. Grow old and live ninety years." Amalya pulled fresh sheets from her cart, and I moved to the opposite side of the bed to help. On my previous two visits, we'd argued about my helping make the bed, but she now seemed content to let me assist. She flicked the fitted sheet across the bed to unfurl it. "How was Nutcracker ballet you saw last time?" she asked.

"Excellent. Very beautiful."

Amalya ducked her eyes bashfully as she ran her hands across the sheet to get the wrinkles out. "You may not believe it, but I was once ballet dancer in my home of Olissa. I danced Nutcracker. Swan Lake. All the big ballets."

My heart danced, giddy at her admission. We'd spoken about ballet during my last two visits, but this was the first time she'd mentioned her career. She was finally opening up.

"Of course, I can believe that," I said, smiling wide as I took the offered top sheet. "You still have a dancer's body and posture. I bet you were great."

Amalya looked up, her eyes glistening. She nodded. "Thank you. I do not talk about ballet much. It is too hard. But you are lovely girl. Easy to talk to."

Part of me wanted to leap across the bed and give her a giant hug as I let the truth of my identity spill from my lips. But I was only batting 50/50 with my adventures in truth telling.

"You're easy to talk to too," I said, following Amalya as she pulled the bedspread back over the sheets. "Very easy. It feels like I've known you forever."

Amalya laughed as she tugged her cart toward the bathroom. "You remind me of my daughter."

I nearly tripped over my own feet. "You have children? Grandchildren?" I asked, dying to hear more about my mother, my brothers, myself.

"A daughter and two grandsons. They live in Jersey."

Handing her a stack of fresh towels from the cart, I ducked my head to hide a frown I couldn't squelch. Was she lying so I wouldn't pity her? Or was it too painful to admit her daughter was dead, her grandsons in prison, her granddaughter essentially given away? My yearning to hug her was now stronger than ever. I ached to tell her she was not alone with her pain. I shared it too. Surely a burden shared together was better than one endured alone?

There was a vice on my heart as I watched Amalya work. It squeezed tighter and tighter until I could barely breathe. As much as I wanted to share Amalya's burden, I could never be more to her than what I was right now, a friendly stranger who visited her hotel.

A silence hung in the air as Amalya worked. I tried to think of a conversation point, but nothing seemed right. Five minutes passed, then ten. Amalya finished the bathroom and started to vacuum. I sat cross-legged on the bed trying not to look like I was watching her every move. Finished with the vacuuming, Amalya stopped and patted my arm. "You are such a sweet girl. Are you coming back to hotel soon?"

My arms twitching with a desire to hug her, I clasped them behind my back. I nodded, finding a smile. "Very soon." With Perun after me, I really shouldn't be visiting anymore, but maybe one more time wouldn't hurt? It was a very big hotel after all.

"See you soon, Lara," said Amalya, smiling, her eyes crinkling in a merry way. She was every bit the picture of a beautiful grandmother. As she turned for the door, I realized it was now or never.

Wait one sec," I called, reaching in my pocket for the ballet ticket. "I um … I have a ticket for La Sylphide tonight at Lincoln Center but can't go." My heart thudded uncomfortably as I rushed to get the words out. "Would you like it?" The ticket was for five rows in front of where Martine and I would sit (me in disguise, of course), and I longed to watch Amalya marvel at the allure of La Sylphide.

Amalya cocked her head to the side and studied me. I stood completely still, not even blinking. Did she see Milena? Did I want her to? Abandoning her cart, she walked over and paused only a few feet away. I couldn't read her at all. Couldn't tell what she saw or what her response was going to be.

"Is it okay to hug you?" she asked. I blinked in rapid fire, then nodded, too dumbstruck to speak. "Thank you," she said, slipping her arms under mine in a soft, tentative hug. "You are very nice for offering the ticket. One of nicest people in a long time."

Realizing my arms hung stupidly at my sides, I wrapped them around her and propped my chin on her shoulder. She smelled the same as I remembered. Like cinnamon and lavender, just like my mom. Wanting more than our cautious embrace, I tightened my grip, drawing her near. I did so slowly, not wanting to frighten her, asking along the way if this was okay. I found her accepting, needy even and wondered how often she got a hug. I hoped this was one of many but feared it wasn't. The hug ended all too quickly, my hands trailing after her as she pulled away.

"Thank you for ticket offer very much. But sorry, I cannot take. I have book club, and I am in charge of discussion. You are so nice for offering, though." She touched my cheek, same as when I was a child, and I leaned in, remembering her. My mother. Olissa.

"No problem," I said, easily mustering a smile. "Maybe next time." Although I was disappointed she couldn't come, I would trade a trip to the ballet for that hug any day.

Amalya smiled and nodded, returning to her cart and opening the door. "See you soon."

"Looking forward to it," I called as the door clicked shut.

Clutching the ballet ticket, I sprawled on the bed; a ridiculous smile plastered on my face. When Amalya looked at me, I could swear she was seeing her granddaughter. She didn't recognize me outright, but she saw something in me that was Milena.

If she could see it, then surely I could be it.

I would be it.

I was Milena Rokva.

# SEVEN

AFTER CHECKING OUT of the hotel, I headed downtown to meet up with my cobbler, Leon. Despite my promise to Albert, contacting Isra was still on my agenda. I knew her Friday schedule and thanks to Leon, one of the best passport and driver's license forgers I'd seen, I now had Isra's new identity as Casey Lamont, in hand. The real Casey, a twenty-five-year-old secretary, had recently died in a car crash in a small Texas border town, leaving her social security number and identity ripe for the taking. "Beautiful work," I said, studying Isra's passport photo. I'd snapped the shot a couple of days ago when she was leaving work, and thanks to a little Photoshop magic, Leon had changed the background to standard passport white. The photo and passport looked legit. I handed Leon an envelope of cash.

"Need anything else Lara," he winked, using the name he'd given me.

"I may need an identity for someone else in a few weeks. I'll be in touch."

Leon nodded, stuffing the envelope into the drawer of his desk "You know where to find me." Leon wasn't your typical movie cobbler working out of a cigar or hat shop backroom. Nope. The best cobbler in all of New York was a sixteen-year-old, genius, criminology major at NYU. What next, tween assassins? At eighteen, I was starting to look and feel a little old for my job.

"That, I do," I said, letting myself out. I had half an hour to get across town before Isra's yoga class ended. I planned to make contact at the juice bar she and her friends routinely hit up afterward.

Although Albert wanted me to steer clear of my fellow cadets, I was tired of following them around and waiting to see something useful. That might take months, or years even. The longer it took, the more likely it was I'd be caught, and although Maxim wasn't a friend, Isra was. Why shouldn't we have a face-to-face? I knew Varos had contacted those cadets he could, to warn about the fissure within Perun, but both Isra and Maxim were still in play. He either contacted them, and they didn't believe him, which wasn't a stretch given his mental state, or he had to run before he could reach them. Besides Varos, Isra had been my best friend. I knew I could trust her to at least hear me out. The fake IDs from Leon were my form of a goodwill gesture. Informing on Perun was dangerous, and I wanted her to know I would look out for her. I'd help her in any way I could.

I made good time despite the traffic going from Leon's NYU dorm to Isra's yoga studio in Midtown East, and I lucked into a parking space on the same street as the juice bar. Tapping my fingers against the steering wheel, I waited for Isra to emerge. My eyes darted a circle between the yoga studio, the clock on the dash, and the street in front of me to check for hidden dangers. If Isra had a tail, I wanted to know about it. Albert and I had never spotted a tail, but I couldn't afford to get sloppy.

A crowd of high-gloss, twenty and thirty-year-old women began to file out of the studio, wearing trendy workout clothes and bouncing ponytails. *Please let today not be the day Isra changes her schedule.*

As if on cue, Isra emerged with her two BFFs, Jane Morgan, a curvy, brunette trophy wife and Mia Kane, a lithe, redheaded, soon-to-be trophy wife. Although both women were good looking, they paled in comparison to Isra. With wavy, golden hair to her waist and dewy, porcelain skin, Isra was a bombshell. Giggling like schoolgirls, the three women walked across the street to the juice bar. I waited five minutes then followed, giving the street one last appraisal for any lurkers.

I joined the line at the counter and surveyed the room from behind my sunglasses. I'd staked it out previously but did a quick reassess for any changes. There were two exits—one in the front, one in the rear. The bar held twenty people—all women. I could identify no immediate dangers on first appraisal and the items I could use as weapons, should the need arise, included the paring knives behind the counter, the chrome bar stool legs, the glass blender jugs and the pot of steaming coffee brewing in the corner. Isra and her friends sat at a table in the back, sipping juice and scrolling through their phones.

Reaching the front of the line, I ordered a concoction called the Turbo with a bunch of fruits and wheat grass then weaved my way to a table opposite Isra's. I popped my sunglasses up to reveal my mismatched eyes, then swung my purse down onto the table with a thunk, trying to draw Isra's attention.

Apparently Isra's Facebook, email or twitter was utterly engaging because she gave me not so much as a glance, forcing me to consider alternative ways of getting her attention. I just needed her to look at me. Once she saw the eyes, she'd know. I'd thought of different scenarios for getting her attention before arriving, from an overly loud phone conversation to complimenting her outfit. I was fidgeting in my seat, mulling things over when my chair emitted a tiny screech as it scraped across the floor. And there it was … the perfect attention getter. What draws more attention than a sound like nails on a chalkboard? Keeping my weight on it, I pushed my chair backward, resulting in an ear-piercing grind that would make anyone cringe.

Bingo. Isra winced and glanced my way. I opened my eyes wide and made an apologetic oops face. "Sorry," I called out to the room.

Isra smiled and returned to perusing her phone. For a second, my identity didn't register, but then it clicked, and she whipped her gaze back to mine. Her breath caught for a second before a mask fell over her face.

I nodded, and Isra ducked her eyes signaling she understood. For the next twenty minutes, I pretended to read my e-reader while Isra gabbed with her friends and showed off some pictures on her phone. Jane and Mia went squee every time Isra scrolled to show something new. There were lots of 'that's so sweet' and one 'oh my god, is that what I think it is.' Isra only nodded and smiled. What in the world were they looking at?

When the group made motions to leave, I got up and headed out ahead of them. I walked half a block and started to window shop, keeping an eye on the door. Isra emerged a few minutes later and exchanged hugs with her friends before heading in my direction. Without a sideways glance, she walked past me and kept on walking. Ten blocks and several random turns later, Isra strolled past the two giant stone lions flanking the NYC Library on 5th Avenue in

Midtown and went inside. I watched from the doors as she scanned the library map then headed for the stairs. I followed, clutching my bag with Isra's new passport and driver's license.

Our tennis shoes squeaked on the floor as we stomped up the stairwell, separated by a couple flights of stairs. After all these years, we were about to talk again. When I'd discovered her picture in the magazine over a year ago, I'd longed to hear her voice, her photo stirring up memories of a sisterhood I missed. I took to having conversations with her in my head and now that it was going to happen for real … well … the young girl who still lurked somewhere inside of me felt giddy. Like I was about to have a sleepover with an old friend not a clandestine meeting of spy operatives.

That said, I knew I had to pair my giddiness with a large helping of caution. Perun might have warned Isra about me, and if that was the case, I'd need to convince her I was in the right and Perun in the wrong. If I couldn't get through to her, then Albert would have an opportune chance to say 'I told you so,' potentially over my grave. I prayed our old childhood bond still held despite years of distance.

Five flights up, I heard the door open and close. I sucked in a breath and rounded the corner. I was doing the right thing. I would find some way to convince her. I had to. Opening the door, I caught a glimpse of golden hair disappearing down an aisle of books and saw Isra's yoga bag dumped beside a table. I walked past Isra's aisle and kept going until I reached the wall, checking for anyone hidden among the stacks. Each row was empty. Apparently, texts on ancient civilizations were not a big draw. Still, I felt edgy about our location. The bag Isra left in the common area was throwing me. Was she signaling her location in the stacks to someone following us? Had I missed a tail? I made my way toward

Isra and turned down the aisle behind hers. My heart was beating a mile a minute. I could see parts of Isra's frame through the bookcases, a bit of hair here, her nose and lips there.

I pulled out a book and pretended to look through it. "Isra," I whispered.

There was a long pause as Isra sank to her knees, pretending to scan a lower shelf. "Milena, what are you doing here? How'd you find me? Are you in trouble?"

"Why'd you leave your gym bag by the tables?" I asked, caution coming first, pleasantries later.

Isra pulled out a book and sat on the floor. "Perun monitors my phone. Even if I turn it off, they can hear me. Doesn't technology make life grand?"

"Makes a girl long for the Cold War, when spying was simple."

"It does," said Isra, her voice wary. "Why are you here? Did Varos send you?"

"Varos? He's contacted you?"

"A month ago. I'm assuming he contacted you, too."

"He did. Did you not believe him about the fissure? Because—"

Isra laughed, the tone sad rather than merry. "Oh, I believed him. He was hanging on by a thread, but I believed him."

I sank to the floor. "Isra, I'm here because I need information about your contacts. I want to take Perun down for what they did to us." I pulled out the clean IDs and shoved them through to her side of the bookcase. "They're solid and will get you anywhere you want to go."

The IDs stayed where they laid. A hard silence hung in the air as Isra pushed a scrap of paper across to my side. At least I thought it was scrap until I turned it over and saw the telltale black and white of a sonogram. Even if I couldn't read it, I knew what it was. Isra peered at me through a gap in the books, a tear wobbling on the edge of her eyelid, ready to fall. "There's a reason I didn't disappear when Varos told me about Perun."

"This is what you were showing your friends on your phone?" I asked.

She nodded.

"It doesn't mean you shouldn't leave. It means you should. And as quick as you can."

"I love my fiancé," whispered Isra. "I tried not to, but I do."

I ran a finger over the image of Isra's baby. "Does he know? Does Perun?" I asked, my voice cracking. A little life that hadn't yet met the world was in the crosshairs of some very dangerous people. When I took on the role of a spy, I'd vowed never to have children. Ever. But Isra probably didn't have a choice. Valentine ops were often told to bait their traps with a baby.

"Yes, on both accounts." She sighed. "I'm sorry Milena, but I can't help you, not with my baby on the line."

I pushed the IDs farther toward her. "You don't have to help me. You can just run. Protect yourself and the baby."

She shook her head. "It's too risky. They'll find me. Running solo would be hard, running with a baby in tow would be impossible. Staying put is the safest thing. Perun doesn't expect much from me. I can keep fulfilling my role."

"They lied to us. You won't be working to help Olissa. You'll just be helping line the pockets of people we never met, leaders we don't know the names of. Perun has put cadets in key sectors of the world's energy markets as economic hitmen. They're going to strangle the supply. Countless will suffer. It's information about your future husband's work with the Federal Energy Commission that Perun has asked for, isn't it?"

A steady flow of tears snaked down Isra's cheeks. "I don't care. I know I should, but I don't." She shook her head and with a deep, gulping breath she found my eyes. "They used us. They took our childhood, but I'm not going to let them have anything else. I want a life even if I have to do the wrong thing to get it." Isra reached through the stacks with her hand. I thought she wanted her photo, so I handed it to her, but she grabbed my hand instead. "I'm so sorry Milena. I know I must be a disappointment to you. I just can't take the risk. I'm not strong like you. I'm not heroic."

She squeezed my hand, and I squeezed back, bowing my head to our clasped fingers. I laughed, a short, hard little laugh. "I'm hardly heroic."

Isra gently pulled free to run her fingers over my cheek and through my hair like she'd done when we were little, after one of Mistress' drunken attacks. At her touch, tears swelled in my eyes. After all these years, it still felt so familiar. So comfortable. "You should let it all go, too. We were pawns in an adult's game. You should live your life for you. Whatever that means. Find something that you love and do it. Find someone to love and don't let go. We put our time in, and now we should live for us and no one else."

I swiped at my tears trying to stuff my emotions back down. "The person I love hates me, and I can't dance. At least not at the level I dreamed of achieving. I've lost too many years of training."

Isra ran her thumb over my cheekbone. "You're young. You still have years to discover what drives you, but you have to be open to it. And true love … that will come too. Someday, someone will see into your soul and love all of you, no matter what." Isra laughed silently. "For better or worse."

"And your fiancé sees into your soul? He loves all of you?"

With one final caress, Isra pulled her hand back through the stacks. Someone was coming. There were clipped heels on linoleum, muffled speech, a high-pitched whine. Isra and I studied our books trying to look busy as a scholarly man in tweed strolled past, an indignant toddler in tow. "Daddy, I want my Lego."

"He sees and knows all the bits of me that matter," whispered Isra, a few seconds after the man passed. We could still hear the disgruntled toddler stomping his feet and blowing raspberries.

"What about the spy bits of you?"

"Those parts aren't the real me. They're not the parts that matter."

"I don't know if I can separate the spy part from the rest. I'm fighting to be Milena when I don't know who she is."

Isra glanced at her watch and put her book back on the shelf. "I'm sorry, I have to get to the gallery. You'll find that girl I knew. I know you will. I see her in you." Isra peered at me over the books and smiled. "I've missed you, Milena. Be safe."

Without a goodbye, Isra walked down the aisle, grabbed her gym bag and disappeared into the library, a protective hand over her belly.

I grabbed the envelope with her IDs and pocketed it. I understood Isra's decision to stay. To live her life, even if that meant being Anna. Parts of being Lex Gastone had been a blessing. But I couldn't do what she was doing, and not just because the real Alexandra was alive and well. A gnawing fire burned inside me to take action. To seek justice against those who wronged me. I couldn't stomach living in a world where Perun got away scot-free. It would eat me alive. I couldn't walk away. Not yet. I had too many unanswered questions and too much anger boiling inside. Perun made sure the last seven years of my life were a lie and left me with almost nothing. No Grant, no Princeton, no career prospects. I didn't really even have Albert anymore. I had one friend. She was an awesome friend, but still.

Living for me … well, that was taking down Perun. Maybe one day my life would be about finding peace and happiness, but that wasn't going to be today or tomorrow. I hoped it would be someday but knew the odds weren't in my favor.

I was okay with that as long as I went down swinging.

# EIGHT

LATER THAT DAY, Martine threw herself dramatically into a booth at Joe's Diner. "I can't believe you drove us around sightseeing for an hour before finally parking. The Bronx isn't exactly scenic, and my stomach's about to eat itself."

"Eat itself? Really?" I grabbed a menu from the stack in the corner. I'd driven around for an hour to make sure we had no tail. Martine was a known friend of mine and seeing her was a risk. A slight one but still a risk. To prepare for an in-person meeting, I'd followed Martine on several occasions looking for tails, and when Martine and Amélie were out, I swept their house for bugs. The way I figured it, Martine could offer me very little strategically; she was just a typical teenager, so the CIA should not consider her as someone I was likely to contact. Still, I wanted to be cautious, for both our sakes.

Seeing Martine's concern after I swept her for bugs and put her phone in a lead bag to block its signal from tracking devices, I didn't want to freak her out further by openly searching for a tail. To hide my intentions, I'd lamely babbled on about the history of architecture in the Bronx. If Martine fact-checked anything I said, she'd bust me pretty quick.

Martine swiveled around in her seat, taking in the diner, her head scanning to and fro like windshield wipers. Subtle she was not. "So where is your Gran?" she whispered.

I nodded to the window. "Across the street at the coffee shop."

"WTF? Then why aren't we over there? Is the food better here or something?"

"The best way to watch someone and not be seen is from a distance."

Martine nodded and smiled. "M, hanging with you is like being at Quantico or The Farm. I love—" Martine abruptly broke off with a wink as the waitress arrived. She was enjoying this way too much.

I ordered a cheeseburger, fries and coke with chocolate cake for dessert and Martine ordered three different slices of pie—lemon meringue, chocolate silk, and Boston cream.

"Are you jonesing for diabetes?" I asked.

Martine snorted. "Look who's talking Miss two-thousand-calorie dinner. Are you starting on the freshmen fifteen, already?"

I laughed. It felt beyond good to be hanging out with Martine. Sure she was a little over excited about the whole spy thing with her winks and whispers, but she was still the same old Martine. "I'm going for a new look. Chunky. It's a disguise."

Martine's mouth fell open. "Really?"

I shook my head, still giggling. "Ah no. I missed lunch today."

"Well, I like your new hair. Black curls suit you."

I ran a hand through my hair and then shook it out model style. "It's good for a wig, isn't it?"

"No shit, that's a wig?"

"Yep," I said, twirling the ends. My gaze shifted to the coffee shop as Amalya and her book-clubbers entered and sat at the table I reserved for them by the window. "There she is," I said, scooting across the booth. I had to stop myself from pressing my nose to the glass like a kid. "She's in the red sweater."

"I see the resemblance," said Martine, peering out the window. "She's a hot tamale."

I smiled. "She is, isn't she?" I took Martine's hands in between mine. "Good Lord, I've missed you so much!"

"Awe, sweetie, I've missed you too. How have things been? You look ... tired."

I waved away her comment. After failing miserably with Isra, I'd gone back to the safe house and stared at the ceiling for several hours. Despite the relative inactivity, I was completely zapped, mentally and physically. If one of my oldest friends wouldn't help me, then what chance did I have with Maxim, who was merely an acquaintance? Without an inside source, I was never going to bring down Perun or get the immunity deal for Albert and me. Maybe it was time to call in Varos? It's not like he was batshit crazy. His was more of a subtle, nuanced crazy. "I'm doing fine. I'm sorry for dragging you here tonight. I know I promised the ballet."

Martine shrugged. "I like the ballet, but I also like pie. I'm good. Besides, who doesn't love a good stalking?"

"I'm not stalking."

"Uh, yes. You most certainly are, but it's cool. I understand. Albert's away, you're living alone, and she's your Gran. You want to feel close to someone. You lived for seven years knowing nothing about how your family was doing; they were virtually lost to you. It makes sense you'd want to get to know her again. I can't believe she turned down the ballet ticket for book club, though."

I frowned. "She's leading the discussion." Was I stalking my grandmother? Was I that pathetic? I'd told myself I was checking in on her, making sure she was doing okay after the move from Olissa and losing her grandsons to prison. I shifted my gaze to the coffee shop and saw Amalya flicking through her book. She had sticky tabs sticking out at odd angles. I'd give a lot to be over there chatting with her and her friends.

"Do you think you'll tell her soon?" asked Martine.

I shook my head, pulling my attention back. "Not until we take care of Perun. It's too dangerous. I need to stop watching … stalking her, too."

Martine nodded, and I shifted focus back to Amalya. She was laughing at something, a big hearty laugh. She'd cleaned my hotel room three times, but I'd never gotten her to laugh like that. Not even close. "I think I may need to leave Albert," I said, glancing at Martine.

Her eyes went wide. "What? Why?"

"I just think it would be best for both of us," I shrugged. "We need to move on." Martine didn't know the real Alexandra Gastone was alive or that Albert was in Olissa to extract her. What she didn't know about Albert couldn't hurt him. Despite Martine knowing who I was, I still had so many secrets. It made conversation way too hard sometimes. I wondered why I'd even brought it up.

"But you need each other. You're family."

"We're not, though. And Albert's getting old. He should be retiring and not trying to bring down foreign spy rings. It's dangerous."

Martine frowned and looked like she was gathering herself for another attack on my reasoning when our food and drinks arrived.

"Perfect timing," I told the waitress, shooting Martine a

look.

Martine shook her head disgusted, but only sighed as she picked up a fork and surveyed her three slices of pie. "We'll talk about this later."

"Sure thing," I said, picking up my gargantuan burger. Greasy deliciousness oozed down my hand, which I licked at unabashed. Yum!

Martine laughed. "Albert would be sad to see your manners have gone to shit."

I cleared another rivulet of grease with my tongue. "Good thing he's not here right now."

"Savage," said Martine, her mouth stuffed with lemon meringue.

"Look who's talking?" I countered, biting into my burger. I chewed and mostly swallowed before shifting the conversation onto Martine. I didn't know why I 'd brought Albert up. I shouldn't have. "How's school and Sadie?"

Martine's mouth twisted into an *oh crap* look. "Sadie and I broke up. I would have told you but with the whole Grant thing ..."

I dropped my fork. "What? Why? You guys were perfect together."

"It just wasn't working. She didn't get me."

"She didn't?"

Martine downed a heaping forkful of Boston cream and shook her head. "Let's face it, what's the likelihood the only two out-and-proud lesbians in my high school are soul mates. We dated because it was easy and because we're good friends."

"And you're still friends?"

"Yep. We got out while the gettin' was good! So … um … you haven't said anything about how things went with Grant other than it being over?"

I pushed my half-eaten burger away and slid the cake over. "And I'm not going to." I shot Martine a look that said not to push as I buried my fork into the cake. I wasn't thinking about Grant. I'd taken a risk, and it hadn't panned out, end of story. At least I wasn't left wondering, *what if*.

"Got it," said Martine, grabbing her plate and swiping a finger across to pick up the remaining film of chocolate.

"Savage," I said, bursting into laughter. "Amélie would be horrified."

Martine grabbed her second plate and did the same with a cackle. She arched an eyebrow. "Good thing she's not here."

The waitress shot us a dirty look, but I chose to ignore it. Tonight was for Martine and me. No one else. If we wanted to be silly and uncouth then so be it.

Martine and I spent the rest of Amalya's book club chatting about random, non-emotion-evoking things like clothes and video games.

"So are we going to stalk her all the way home?" asked Martine, as the book club packed up. "Ork could probably use a walk."

I sighed, my shoulders sagging. The obvious answer was no, but that didn't sit well with me. "You're my witness. This is the last night I'm going to stalk my grandmother."

Martine flashed a knowing smile. "So that would be a yes then."

I nodded. "We won't walk, though. We'll just drive by her apartment on the way back into the city. If anyone is watching Amalya, a three-legged Scottish Deerhound will be a dead giveaway I'm around."

Martine shook her head. "Jeez, you have to think of so much stuff all the time just to be safe. You're amazing."

I snorted. "Hardly." I was playing fast and loose with the rules of being a spy what with my current dinner date companion and tailing Amalya. I needed to stop taking so many chances. And I would. Soon.

We paid our check and ambled to the car well after Amalya and her book club crew scattered. I had Amalya's address and didn't need to follow on her heels. We found Ork napping in the back seat, but he promptly yawned and stood, ready to get out for a walk. "Hold on buddy. One quick drive by Amalya's, and we'll stop at a park for you to pee."

Ork cocked his head to the side and whined. I kissed his snout. "I'll be quick, I promise." I did not want Ork having an accident in Albert's car. He was a big dog with a big bladder. His accidents weren't small.

Amalya was out of sight by the time we were loaded and ready to go. I went the scenic route wanting to make sure I had no tail. My focus entirely on my surroundings and any headlights appearing in my rearview mirror, I didn't notice the silence between Martine and I until she broke it. I heard her say something but didn't catch it.

"Sorry. What?" I asked.

"I'm worried about you."

I made a couple more turns. Deeming the coast clear, I turned my focus to Martine. "Sorry," I said, unable to think of a better response. I mean what do you say to that? I guess I could have said, "Don't worry," but that's hardly reassuring.

"Someone our age shouldn't have to worry about bugs, GPS tracking, and tails. That's what you're doing now, right? Making sure we don't have a tail? That's why you were such a chatty Cathy earlier. I knew that building didn't look like a Frank Lloyd Wright."

"Well, it's not like I can do anything about it. I'll have to weather the storm and hope it breaks before I'm dead."

Martine gasped. "That's seriously not funny."

"I wasn't trying to be funny. It's the truth. When you've

lived this life as long as I have, you stop worrying so much about dying. The reaper comes for everyone, eventually. I'm not trying to upset you."

"Well, you are," said Martine, nearly shouting. From the corner of my eye, I could see her body was rigid, her jaw set, her fists balled

"Good grief. Quiet down. I promise I'll live forever, okay?"

Martine grimaced then shoved my shoulder. "You're a jerk you know that?"

I nodded because I did know it. I couldn't seem to help myself these days. I was regularly crabby with Albert over a whole slew of things besides his inability to get my name right, and now I'd upset Martine, my one and only friend.

I turned down Amalya's street. Just one last drive by and then I'd be done. No more hotel visits. No more stalking. The one hug would have to be enough.

Ork started to whine again, needing a walk. I glanced toward Amalya's, hoping to catch a glimpse of her as I pressed my foot to the floor. My attention split between the apartment and the road, I nearly missed seeing a tall man ushering her, not so gently, down the stairwell. "What the hell?"

# NINE

"IS YOUR GRAN getting mugged?" screeched Martine, straining against her seatbelt.

I swerved into an empty parking space on the opposite side of the road. We faced the wrong direction but screw it. "I don't know. Stay here," I said, undoing my seatbelt and hopping out. Ignoring me, Martine was on my heels as I raced forward, hunched low behind the cars. Across from Amalya's apartment, I chanced a glance. Amalya wasn't screaming for help, but even from a distance, I could tell her body was stiff. A large man had her by the arm, but she wasn't fighting him.

"What do you think?" asked Martine.

"I don't think she's getting mugged."

From our position, we could hear muffled conversation. Two tense voices, speaking in sharp, clipped tones. After a few moments, keys jangled and a door creaked open then shut.

I handed Martine my keys. "I'm going to have a look, but I don't want you anywhere near this. There's a park two blocks down and to the right. Take Ork for a pee and I'll meet you—"

"No way am I—"

I shook my head. "Martine, I will meet you over there as soon as I can. If I'm not there in half an hour, you can call the police. But I can't have you here. Not right now." I pulled the gun from underneath my jacket and clicked the safety off. Martine inhaled sharply, her eyes going huge. "Now," I commanded, nodding toward the car. Martine held my gaze for what seemed an eternity. Both fear and amazement filled her eyes. Finally, she nodded, taking off for the car in a crouched run.

I waited until the engine hummed to life and the car pulled from its spot, before slinking across the street to just above the stairwell.

A light flicked on in the living room window of Amalya's apartment. I could see her and the man's back. Amalya's face was pinched and angry. She wagged a finger at him. He came toward her, and she backed away, putting a coffee table between them. What the hell was going on? Who was this guy?

As if on cue Amalya's cat darted out of a corner, and the man's head swiveled so I could see his profile. I promptly reeled backward onto my butt. It wasn't just any man in there with Amalya. It was my father.

I was up a half-second later, peering back through the window. Father had navigated the coffee table and now had Amalya by the wrist. She cried out as he wrenched her arm and raised his other hand as if to hit her. Fearing for Amalya, I started for the door, my gun at the ready. My mind was chaos. What was he doing here? Was he looking for me? I had so many questions about Perun. Would he have the answers? Would he tell me? Did he know anything that was worthy of an immunity deal? He was hurting Amalya, would he try to hurt me if I wasn't careful?

I hadn't seen him since my first day at Compound Perun, but I knew he was somehow messed up with them, and I had no idea how dangerous he might be. Maybe he was the Father I remembered—the one who was tough but never raised a hand to me, then again maybe he wasn't.

I opened my grandmother's front door without knocking. *Ready or not, here I come.*

The door shrieked, and my father swung around, pulling his gun. We eyed each other over our gun sights—a Father and daughter frozen in a time warp—fingers twitching on triggers.

I stepped farther into the room. "Hi, Dad. Amalya, you okay?"

Amalya looked from me to my father and then back again, her face lit up with both surprise and fear. I was wearing a wig, but there was no way she didn't recognize me as the girl from her hotel. Unsteady on her feet, she nodded in reply while sinking into the couch.

"Amalya, it's going to be—"

Amalya's eyes widened, a panic curling her deeper into the couch.

The three of us collectively flinched at a very loud woof, woof, woof. A second later, Ork was at my side, his teeth bared, his feral growl low and guttural. Amalya's cat streaked across the room and up some curtains. At the top, she hissed and spat. Ork ignored her, my dad his sole focus.

Oblivious to the bedlam, Dad narrowed his eyes, "Little O?"

"Yep, it's me," I said, my voice strangely light, like this was all a fun game. It sounded nothing like how I felt inside. What was Ork doing here? Was Martine outside the door? What would I do if she came in? Coiled tight, I could barely breathe. Sweat pricked at my forehead, giving away my nervousness. At least my gun hand wasn't shaking. It was steady. Aimed and ready.

"Well then. I guess I don't need to be asking Amalya if she's seen you," said dad, his gun still raised. "I've been looking all over."

"Is that so?"

"You've caused us a lot of problems. Mistress isn't happy."

"Can't say I'm too sorry about that." I studied my father wishing I could read him better. Did he feel anything at seeing me? Did he know what I'd gone through at Perun because of Mistress? "You said she'd be kind. You said she'd love me."

"Who?"

"Mistress. You said she'd love me." Ork was snarling, slinging slobber onto my pants. I dropped a hand to his head, trying to calm him. "Quiet boy, quiet."

"I remember."

"You lied."

Father raised a puzzled eyebrow. "Did I?"

There was silence for a moment before Amalya spoke, her voice a tiny whisper. "Zakhar, she is your daughter. Milena, he is your father. You must lower your guns."

I glanced at Amalya. She'd aged ten years in only a few minutes. She looked so tired now. Her brightness was gone, replaced by fear. She was afraid of my father but also of me. She shrunk under my gaze. My heart broke. I hadn't wanted this.

Father laughed, pulling a second gun from behind his back and aiming at her. "Tut, tut. Let's not ruin the reunion so soon."

Amalya whimpered and covered her face. Any hope I had that my father wasn't a total bastard evaporated. Amalya was an old woman. There was nothing he could gain from making her cower except a perverse sense of pleasure at the power of it.

"Some reunion," I said. "I'm really feeling the love."

Father continued to glower. "You screwed things up when you didn't take out Vladik," he snarled. "We had him in check, and you surrendered the game."

"He was a man, not a chess piece," I spat. I was no longer Father's Little O. I could see it in his cold, unforgiving eyes. I was nothing more than a Perun cadet. A chess piece who hadn't played by his rules. Instead of being sad about the shift, I was furious. What had happened to him? Perun had stolen him too; I was sure of it. They'd taken all his goodness and left only the dregs.

Zakhar pulled his gun from Amalya and advanced on me.

I stood my ground. I would not cower in front of this man who'd abandoned me. Abandoned himself. Ork's growl deepened and he barked twice—a menace to his voice I'd never heard before.

Zakhar shook his head. "Like always you're not understanding the nuances of the game. That's why you never beat me."

"I was seven when we played. I'm a lot better than I used to be." Playing Albert, I'd won almost half the time, and I'd put money on Albert being smarter than my dad. Daddy dearest didn't know who he was messing with.

Zakhar barked a laugh. "I doubt that. I thought you were at least a useful pawn, but turns out I was wrong." He shook his head, his face pitying. *Poor Little O, she just doesn't understand.* "Vladik betrayed Perun, you foolish girl. All that Perun worked for, it's falling apart because of him and because you chose an old man over your country."

My gun wobbled. "Wait. What?" *Vladik Kasarian, the*

*President of Olissa, was Perun? One of the leaders?* Ork lowered himself ready to lunge. I fumbled for his collar.

"Quiet that three-legged mutt of yours," hissed Zakhar, sighting one gun onto Orkney.

I stepped in front of Ork and waved my gun. "Explain yourse—"

What happened next is a blur.

Ork lunged around me.

A gun erupted.

My heart stopped.

My ears rang.

My lungs tried for air but couldn't find any.

Ork nosedived into the floor as momentum carried him forward, one hind leg giving away. He howled in pain. I howled too. Red seeped from a bullet hole in his thigh.

I turned on Zakhar my trigger finger itching to fire, but he was already on me having used my moment of shock to advance. His gun at my temple, he disarmed me then slid an arm around my neck. "We asked you to kill Vladik, and you abandoned us. Because of you, we had to resort to a lesser option, which also failed thanks to you." Father seethed, his breath fiery. "When Vladik killed his sister Alina and replaced her with Alexandra Gastone, I told my boss he was corrupt, but the fool didn't believe me until Vladik held all the power. Then my daughter is tasked with fixing the problem and what does she do?" Father dug the gun into my head. It shook in his hand with fury. "What does she do? She saves Vladik. She lets the greedy bastard win. That's what she does. To win the game, Little O, you have to be willing to make sacrifices. You should have poisoned Vladik like we asked and used Albert as the scapegoat. Albert Gastone was your test. Your Queen's sacrifice. But you failed. You failed Perun; you failed yourself, and you failed me." With his gun as a guide, Father pushed my eyes toward Ork. My gallant boy was still trying to protect me, shuffling toward my father on his belly, growling with menace. "You're weak. You let your relationships get in the way."

I blinked twice at Ork, my shoulders shaking. If he could be fierce, so could I. I choked out a sob when really there was only fury inside of me. If Father thought I was weak, I would use it to my advantage. I would give him weak, then make him pay.

Taking the bait, Father loosened his grip, and that's when I slammed my head back into his face. My elbow found his ribs. I whipped around and connected with his jaw then grabbed his hand, stripping the gun. My father went for an uppercut, but I blocked. "Run!" I screamed to Amalya.

I landed a right hook and tried for a front kick to the groin. Father sidestepped and made a grab for my foot, but I was too fast. I came at him with another swing, my fury giving me speed and power. Out of the corner of my eye, I could see Amalya hadn't moved. "Run," I yelled again. "Get out of here."

I landed a few more punches, one to the gut and one to the face before getting hit with a bell-ringer that made my knees wobble. Knowing I would be finished if he landed another one, I lunged forward and hit him with my shoulder, sending both of us to the ground. On top, I hit Father's ears like they were percussion cymbals. Having been on the receiving end of the same move in training, I knew the pain it caused was excruciating. Father howled as I leaped up. I darted for the gun then dashed to Amalya. "Come on," I said, grabbing a hand, trying to tow her forward. She needed to move so I'd be free to help Ork.

Amalya's eyes fell to the gun. "Come on, we have to go," I said again. She yanked her hand from mine and shrunk back into the couch.

"Get away from me," she choked. "Get away."

Taking a new tact, I held my hand out to her. "I won't hurt you. I prom—"

Amalya suddenly cringed, and I turned just in time to see Father lunging for me, his face glazed with hatred. We careened into the couch, narrowly missing Amalya. I threw elbow after elbow, but only a few landed. Father grabbed a fist full of my wig and whipped me backward. My wig came free, but I was already off balance and Father got an arm around my neck. I flailed, my legs spinning, trying to gain purchase. I swung my gun hand backward and pulled the trigger, hoping to hit him in the leg. I missed the first time as he muscled me across the room, but from his scream, I hit something the second. Still, he didn't fall. Before I could try again, I was pressed against a nearby wall. Grabbing my gun hand, he hit it against the wall until the gun clattered free. Taking my hair again, he smashed my head against the wall, then snaked his arm around my neck making it hiss with fire. He hauled me backward toward the door. I raked my nails over his arm, trying to break free as blackness crept in. *Air. I need air.* I pulled. I scratched. My hands grew slick with his blood. Still his grip was firm. I flailed for his face and scoured his cheeks, drawing more blood. Within seconds, he had me out the door and up the stairwell, my legs spinning under me. *What was the plan? Take me back to Perun? Punish me? Ork needed help; I couldn't leave him.*

Out of nowhere there was the clang of metal on metal. "Stop," barked a voice. "Police."

Father's arm loosened as he swiveled to identify the point of danger. Using the opportunity, I found my feet and pushed off, flinging myself backward. Losing his footing, Father fell, and I rolled over the top of him and out of his grasp.

From a darkened alley, Martine appeared with a gun in her unsteady hands. *Where did Martine get a gun?* I ran toward her, and she fumbled it into my hands. I turned it on Father as he scrambled to stand.

Father cocked his head to the side and raised his hands. "You wouldn't kill your own father would you?" he asked, voice calm.

"You shot my dog," I said, pulling the trigger.

Click. Click. Click.

My gaze dropped from my father to the gun in disbelief.

Click.

Click.

Click.

"No," I wanted to scream. "No. No. No."

Martine had handed me an unloaded gun. My insides burned with rage as a wicked smile played across my father's face. I bent low readying myself for another attack, but he only laughed a hearty belly-shaker like we'd just shared a joke. He laughed at my useless gun then turned and walked away. No, he didn't walk. He strutted. He strutted away like nothing of consequence had happened.

I could have bolted after him. I would have, if not for Orkney. As Father rounded the corner, I raced back down the stairs and into Amalya's apartment.

# TEN

THE DOOR STILL open, I ran past Amalya, who sat frozen on the couch. "Do you have any bandages?" I asked, kneeling by Ork. I kissed him on the snout. "You're going to be okay, buddy. I love you. I love you so much. Why did you have to be so brave?" Taking off my jacket, I put gentle pressure on the wound, causing Ork to whimper. He was bleeding, but it wasn't terrible. The bullet hadn't hit an artery, thank God.

My grandmother still hadn't moved. "Amalya, I don't mean to scare you or to be rude, but do you have bandages? If so, I need them. Now!"

She finally nodded, getting up, but a second later she sat back down as Martine came tentatively down the stairs and through the door. Assessing the room and finding it free of gun-wielding madmen, Martine dashed to my side.

"Now Amalya," I said again.

She scampered into what I guessed was her bedroom. I could only hope she was going after bandages and didn't plan to barricade herself inside.

"Oh my God, M, what just happened? When I heard a gun go off inside your Gran's apartment, I freaked."

I stared down at her gun, which now lay at my side. "Why'd you give me an unloaded gun?" I hissed, my anger flaring.

"What happened?" asked Martine, ignoring my question.

"He shot Ork. He shot him like it was nothing. And when I tried to shoot him with your gun ... well ... you know what happened." Why hadn't Father come after me again? Why walk away when all I had was a useless gun? Was he worried about the cops coming? About being seen fighting me out in the open? An older man brawling with a teenage girl might draw a crowd. Locals might step in and try to help me. Was that it? It seemed wrong but maybe ...

"It's my fault," whispered Martine. "He bolted as soon as I opened the door. I tried to grab him ..."

With my free arm, I pulled her into a half-hug. "Please, don't blame yourself. My dad is to blame. No one else. You got it?"

Martine sucked in a phlegmy breath and hugged me back. I'm also pretty sure she wiped her nose on my shirt, but I was past the point of caring. "Got it."

Returning, Amalya knelt beside me and tore open the packets of bandages. When I lifted my jacket, she tended to Ork without my asking. "It is okay, sweetheart. Looks like only a flesh wound."

"We need to get out of here," I said. "Someone might have heard the gunshots. Amalya, do you have a blanket we can put Ork on to carry him?"

She nodded, snatching one off the nearest couch. She laid it out, and Martine and I slid Ork onto it as best we could.

Preparing to leave, Martine picked up her gun with two timid fingers and dropped it into her purse.

"It can't hurt you when it's not loaded," I said, trying but failing to reign in my frustration as a flash of my father's grin and laugh returned. I knew it wasn't Martine's fault.

Not really. I shouldn't have let her anywhere near me, and I'd been all too willing to accept her easy breezy attitude about my being a spy. But his smile. His cackle. They incensed me. "Why bring it at all?"

"Because you're a spy. Being around you isn't exactly the safest thing in the world."

"Where'd you even find a gun?" I asked, leaning down to give Ork one last kiss and a few words of encouragement, then lifting my side of the blanket.

"It's Gran's."

Martine lifted her side, and Amalya put her hands underneath the blanket in the middle to give Ork support. Together we shuffled for the door. Having retrieved my loaded gun, I drew it before reaching the stairs just in case my father had returned.

He hadn't. The sidewalk and street were empty. The street felt sleepy with everyone's lights out, and if I were forced to guess whether the cops were coming, I would have said no. Maybe neighbors assumed the gunfire was from a TV? Maybe they were used to loud arguments that stretched out onto the street? Maybe Amalya's basement apartment helped to muffle the sound? Whatever the reason, I was thankful.

After Ork bolted, Martine had thankfully gotten back in the SUV to chase him down and was now double parked outside Amalya's. We slid Ork into the back seat as carefully as possible. Martine, already in possession of the car keys, nodded at me once then went around to the driver's side, leaving me alone with my grandmother.

"I'm sorry," I said, walking toward her, hoping to give her a quick hug. This was a goodbye … potentially forever.

Amalya threw out a hand. "Please, stop."

I studied her, confused. There was an emptiness inside me that craved her scent … touch … embrace, even if it was only for a second. Why wouldn't she give it to me? "I was trying to protect you. I'd never hurt you."

Amalya shook her head, her faced pained. "No. I cannot. You must go, please."

"Gran, I don't understand. I've missed you so much. I may never see you again. Please, I have to hurry."

Her lips twisted as if she fought a grimace. "I cannot forgive you. I know it is wrong. You were only small child. But I cannot. Not after what your mother did. After what she took from me."

I blinked at her trying to understand. "Forgive me? What did Mother do?"

Amalya strained forward, not moving her feet, and patted my shoulder twice. Pat. Pat. It felt like something you might give a dog when you hate dogs. "You will not come to hotel again. Okay? No more."

Amalya didn't wait for a reply. I stared dumbstruck as she retreated down the stairs and closed the door. I flinched as the deadbolt clicked into place, securing her inside and away from me. *What had I done?*

# ELEVEN

I WOKE WITH a start, jumping to my feet. Someone had touched me. My hands came up to protect myself before my eyes even opened. When they did open, I winced, flailing my arms to shield myself from the harsh fluorescent light of the Emergency Vet waiting room. My eyes burned, dry from crying.

"I got here as soon as I could," said Brad, resting a hand on my shoulder and guiding me back down to the tiny two-seater couch where he'd found me. "How's Orkney?"

Martine and I had rushed Orkney to the nearest open Veterinary office and she'd stayed as long as she could but eventually needed to catch the midnight train back to Fair Valley. The vet stabilized Ork, but he hadn't yet gone into surgery, a golden retriever hit by a car had priority, which I tried to take as a good sign. I'd waited an hour by myself, but eventually, the loneliness I worked so hard to keep at bay with Albert gone, came on like a bullet train, flattening me. I called Brad in a moment of desperation. Ork was my rock, and now he was hurt because of me. Because he was brave and my father was evil.

"He's waiting for surgery," I said, fighting the constriction in my throat. More tears wanted to come, but I was empty.

"What happened?" He put a hand to my cheek then quickly darted it away as if I'd burned him. Did I suddenly have leprosy? Why could no one bear to touch me? "I'm hoping the other guy looks worse?"

Dark purple bruises bloomed large on my head and jaw; my hair was matted and sticking every which way, and mascara streaked my face. If it were Halloween or the apocalypse, I'd easily pass for a zombie. "No. Unfortunately not."

Waiting on Brad to arrive, I told myself I'd be stoic. No emotions. No tears. No breakdown. I put up a wall. One I hoped would be strong enough to protect me. My dad called me weak, and I didn't want it to be true. *Be strong. Keep it together Lex, keep it tog—ah shit. Damn it.* How could I expect Albert to remember my name when even I couldn't? *Shit.*

Brad felt too close, so I threw an arm out to push him away. God, I was so messed up. I was lonely, so I called him, and now that he was here I needed space. Every fiber of my being wanted to kick or punch something. To lash out. I needed to feel physical pain rather than emotional. I dug my fingernails into my arm, almost crying out with relief as tiny threads of pain corkscrewed from the points of contact. Brad saw me and grabbed my hand, pulling it free.

"Don't," he said. I would have protested more, but we weren't the only ones in the waiting room. The Labrador's family sat huddled together in the opposite corner.

"It was my father," I whispered. "He shot Ork. He tried to kill me." The thought shook me to my core. Where had the father I knew gone?

*I am strong. I am strong. I am strong.* I repeated the mantra over and over in my head, trying to regain my composure.

It didn't work.

A tearless sob broke free, as I curled into myself.

I was so damn tired; I didn't know if I could keep doing this. Keep fighting. My father had foolishly revealed valuable intel on the leaders of Perun. It was information I could use to bring them down, but what would I lose if I did? Perun wouldn't go down without a fight. There would be casualties. Ork had almost been one of them. Maybe Isra was right, and I should cut my losses and just live, disappear into the crowd and live for me. Who might I lose if I kept going? Albert was getting too old for this sort of thing. And what about Alexandra? I'd need her help to take down Vladik. Albert couldn't lose her, not a second time.

Brad put his arm around me and tugged me close. I tried to resist, but he refused to listen. "Don't be silly M. Let me be here for you. I know what Ork means to you." At his words, the last of my fight drained away, and I sank into him. He hugged me tight and let me sob, asking nothing more than to let him be there. "This should never have been your life," he whispered. "You weren't meant for this."

I shuddered, and my stomach dropped. "You think I'm weak, too?" Did everyone see what my father saw?

Brad scoffed, and I jiggled in his arms. "You're hardly weak. No, not at all. Remember I watched you growing up. I know how strong you are and what you had to endure. All I meant was you were meant for something other than a spy's life. Trust me, I know a lot of spies, and you're not like any of them." Brad pointed at my heart. "You're more of an artist than a chess player. Albert showed me some of your English assignments. They were always so clever and unique. You'd turn things on their head like when you made Snow White into the bad guy and the queen into the good."

His words thawing me, I tucked my head in under his chin. Part of me wanted to rebel at being held like a child by a guy I barely knew. But the other part needed the comfort. My world had imploded. Again.

# TWELVE

I FELL ASLEEP lulled by Brad's warmth and woke some time later with a chill, Brad gone. He'd laid his coat over me, but it wasn't the same as body heat. My eyes darted around the waiting room until I saw Brad. He stood at the reception counter tapping on his phone. Was he texting Albert about my breakdown? That was all Albert needed. He was worried enough already. Brad had done a lot for me, and I accepted the comfort he offered, but I still didn't trust him. What was he to Albert anyway? I didn't understand their connection. Why was a seventy-year-old CIA analyst best buddies with a twenty-eight-year-old field operative? Albert was cool but still …

"What are you doing?" I asked, walking over. I tried not to sound accusatory, but wasn't sure I succeeded.

"I've just shown Dr. Abrams my credentials and asked him not to report the gunshot wound. I'm also moving money around so I can pay Ork's bill," he said, lifting up the corner of said bill. "Ork's out of surgery. We can go visit now."

Despite being completely spent, the kindness of his gesture filled me with a momentary warmth. Who was this guy? "You don't have to do that. I have money."

Brad shook his head. "Don't worry about it. You can bake me a cake or something as a thank you. Your money is designated for other things."

Brad took my hand, and we followed Dr. Abrams into the back. I didn't realize I was holding my breath until Brad squeezed my hand and told me to "Breathe." Ork was already getting on in years, and I worried he'd look frail now. I didn't know if my heart could take that. After all, he'd been shot trying to protect me. For years, Ork was my only confidant. He was the keeper of my secrets. My best friend.

We found Ork asleep on a dog bed in Abrams' private office. "Given his size, we thought he'd be more comfortable in here than in one of the cages," said Abrams. "We'll need to monitor him for at least a week and do some physical therapy. The bullet missed bone but tore up his thigh muscle pretty bad. With Orkney having only two good legs at the moment, we'll exercise him in one of our swim tanks to build up his strength."

I nodded, sliding down the wall next to Ork. I laid a hand on his head and took a breath. He was warm. Alive. Snoring. "Thank you. Thank you for everything."

Brad sat next to me as Dr. Abrams left. "He's lucky to have such a caring dog mom."

I shook my head. "He's not lucky. He got shot for knowing me. That's some reward for years of loyalty."

"Some things are worth dying for. Ork obviously knew that. He thought you were worth it."

"I'm not."

"I know a few people who would beg to differ, myself included. I've surveilled a lot of people over the years, and you're one of the good ones. Give yourself some credit."

"I was playing a role. I'm a liar. Whatever you saw wasn't

me."

"You weren't guarded all the time. I saw the real you. Not all the time but enough. It's amazing what you can see just by watching."

I cocked an eyebrow. "I hope you know that sounds super creepy."

Brad's lips quirked, and he laughed. "Yes. Yes. It most certainly does, doesn't it?" He nudged my arm. "Sorry."

Ork started to twitch, his eyes opening. I scratched his favorite spot behind his ears with one hand while scratching the base of my neck with another. "Damn Ork. I think you gave me fleas," I said, shivering at the thought but also laughing. I glanced at Brad. "I just want to be normal. I want having fleas to be my biggest worry. I want to get my thrills from skydiving or hang gliding or however regular people get their kicks. I want to go to the shooting range and enjoy having a great eye knowing I'll never have to kill someone with it. I want to study martial arts for fun, not necessity. I don't want to lie anymore. I don't want to hide."

"This won't last—"

I rested a hand on Brad's thigh, stopping him. I studied him for a second. His physique was fine-tuned and combat ready. His eyes were kind but also world-weary. He knew what I was talking about. He knew but liked getting his thrills from the job. We were opposites, but that was okay because I needed him to be exactly who he was, so I could become who I wanted to be … free.

I replayed *the pre*vious night's events and tried to find the right words. I'd somehow managed to get a few hours of sleep, and although my heart still hurt like hell, my mind was clear.

"I'm not telling you this because I need comfort," I said, unable to keep a smile from my face. "I'm telling you because

I'm going to bring down Perun, and I'm hoping you'll want to help me."

Brad's eyes widened, and he nodded for me to continue.

"My father let too much slip last night, and now I know how we can take Perun down. I'm willing to tell you what I learned, but I need your word you won't bring it to the CIA right away. I need you to stay on *vacation*."

Brad frowned. "That's a big ask depending on the information. If American lives—"

"What's Albert to you?"

Brad's brow furrowed. "What do you mean?"

"I mean … what is he to you? You were willing to keep me a secret from the CIA, so I figure he must mean a lot."

"He does."

"Why?"

"He just does. He's like a father to me. He was there when I needed him after my mom died. I don't have any other family."

"So you love him?"

"Yes. Very much."

"Then you'll keep my secret until we can use it to get Albert, Alexandra and me an immunity deal. I need the op to be in motion, so my plan is the CIA's easiest option, and they can't cut us out of the deal."

What I failed to mention was I also wanted to control the information flow coming out of Perun so that I could protect my friends. To do that, I'd need to bring Varos into the fold, but Brad didn't need to know that right now. It was best I left Varos as a last quarter surprise. I just hoped intel on the cadets wasn't a deal breaker for the immunity agreement I wanted to broker.

Brad cocked an eyebrow. "Immunity, huh? You must have something really good."

"Do we have a deal?"

"Fine, it's a deal. Tell me what you have."

"My dad was livid I didn't kill Vladik Kasarian because he's the Perun leader behind the fissure. He took Alexandra under his wing because of her genius and strayed from Perun's vision. If there's a fissure, it means there's also an opposition leader within Perun who my dad is working for, and this got me thinking. I could be wrong, but I'm guessing his half-brother Tarkan is also Perun. That would explain why they never revealed their familial relationship to the public, and why Tarkan jumped into the political arena to run for President against Vladik, despite showing no prior interest in politics. Vladik was grabbing for power both within Perun and Olissa, and Tarkan was trying to stop him."

"You're saying that Vladik Kasarian is Perun and probably Tarkan too?" Brad's voice was cautious as if he couldn't dare to believe it.

"During all my years at Compound Perun, we never learned who the leaders were. They said it was in case we were caught, but now … now we can blow this whole thing up."

"How much do you think we can trust this intel? Your father could have been lying to trap you somehow."

"My gut says the intel's good, and at the very least it's worth checking out."

A broad smile crept slowly across Brad's face.

I smiled back. "We'll need flights to Olissa ASAP."

Brad grunted, understanding where my plan was headed. "Albert's not **going to l**ike it."

"We'll have to make him understand. Using Alexandra to get Vladik is our best bet. Tarkan will be easy. The CIA can check him out and take care of him if needed. But Vladik is President. After the gala, his camp has to be thinking assassination attempt. His security will be heavy. If we infiltrate his computer network with Alexandra's help, we can figure out how he's controlling Perun's network of operatives, and what steps he's taking to control the world energy markets. We can bring both him and Perun down for good."

My heart leaped at the thought.

It danced at the idea of having true freedom.

I could do this.

I would do this.

# THIRTEEN

BRAD BOOKED US on a direct flight to Olissa fifteen minutes after I said a tearful goodbye to Ork, promising to return as soon as I could. I slipped Dr. Abrams an extra big tip to treat Ork like a King while I was gone. He was to spare no expense. My guilt was such I may have made Dr. Abrams promise to give Ork steak twice a week. Two hours later we were at JFK and ten hours after that our plane touched down in Olissa.

I was back home after seven long years.

"There it is," I said, snaking through the crowd at baggage claim and grabbing my hiking backpack. Brad was right behind me, grabbing his.

"How you feeling?" he asked, as we shrugged on our packs and headed to the final customs screening.

I bopped from foot-to-foot trying to contain my energy. I'd spent the plane trip going through our plan. I'd played out different scenarios in my head, looked for weaknesses, and thought of countless Plan B options. I'd been in 'the zone' as far as tactical planning, but as soon as the plane's wheels touched the tarmac, I'd gone from serious to giddy. Despite all we hoped to accomplish and the dangers associated, as I walked off the plane I couldn't contain my excitement about being back in Olissa. For all that I hated Perun, I loved my country—little Olissa, the nation that refused to die, the country that fought her way back into existence after every damn invasion. I flashed Brad a smile. "Good. Really good."

After I successfully made it through Customs, thanks to one of Leon's excellent passports, Brad and I hailed a cab. Brad had informed Albert we were coming to Olissa with new information, and Albert would have happily picked us up, but caution called for a cab to drop us a few streets from his safe house. Brad and I needed to make sure government surveillance hadn't noticed our arrival. Our disguises were first rate, but with the sophistication of facial recognition software, you couldn't be too careful.

To avoid being recognized and to match my passport photo, I wore brown contacts and a long mousy brown wig that shrouded my face. Glasses topped off the ensemble along with a half-inch of makeup to cover my bruises. Brad also wore glasses, a go-to item for every spy, and walked with a hunched, apologetic posture. He'd used inserts to pudge out his cheeks and change the shape of his face. Contrary to the Hollywood standard, it's much better to be an average looking spy than a good-looking one unless you're a Valentine operative. Being noticeable isn't a positive attribute. With our hiking backpacks, we hoped to blend in with the twenty-something, world-traveling crowd who were in Olissa for the beer and the scenery.

It took all my inner willpower not to have my nose pressed to the glass as our cabbie made his way toward the city. In my absence, the city had transformed into something fresh and modern. There was little trace of the crumbling buildings of only seven years ago.

"Olissa's come a long way, hasn't she?" said Brad, noticing my awe.

My heart was a chaotic mix of happy and sad at seeing all Olissa had become. "What will happen to it all?" I whispered, a niggle of worry snaking down my spine. If we managed to take down Kasarian, would Olissa be ruined in the process? Would it fall apart as special interest groups grabbed for power?

Brad's smile fell away. He started to say something then shook his head and shrugged. Neither of us could know what would happen. The outcome depended on a thousand factors we could only guess at knowing. If we were successful, Olissa would, once again, have to fight to save herself. The good of the many outweighed the good of the few. It was either Olissa or the world. If we didn't manage to bring down Kasarian and cripple Perun, every country including the United States would be starved for energy. Economies would sputter and fail, strangled by an energy crisis. "It has to be done," I whispered. "She'll make it through. She always has."

Brad reached over and squeezed my hand. "She's tough like you. She'll make it to the other side, better and stronger."

I clutched Brad's hand and nodded, hoping it was true.

We spent the rest of the cab ride in silence, both on the lookout for any tails. Seeing none, we had the cabbie drop us a couple of blocks from Albert's, outside a large multi-building apartment complex that would take a bazillion years to search if the cabbie were to lead the authorities our way. We waited until the cab was far into the distance before grabbing our packs and setting off for Albert's.

"I didn't give Albert any details when I called. He's not going to like what you have to say, and he's going to balk at involving Alexandra," said Brad. "Do you want to be good cop or bad?"

I hiked my backpack farther up my shoulders and sneaked a look at Brad. By nature, Albert was overly protective of those he loved. He hid me from the CIA for years and wouldn't want to risk Alexandra's safety. I worried about damaging our relationship if I pushed too hard. He might see ulterior motives where there were none. "Um … well …"

Brad laughed. "It's fine. I'm happy to be bad cop. It will be better coming from me, anyway."

Part of me sagged with relief. *Thank God.* But another part, the suspicious part, wondered why Brad thought bad cop would be better coming from him. "Why's that?" I asked.

Brad's eyebrow arched. "Why's what?"

"Why is it better coming from you?"

He shrugged. "Just is. I've known Albert for years. We're colleagues, and he trusts my judgment."

"But he loves me, and I'm his gra ..." I stuttered to a stop. "He loves me," I repeated, trying to cover my slip.

"All the more reason to protect your relationship." Brad grinned wickedly and nudged my arm. "I'm doing you a favor. Don't look a gift horse in the mouth." He reached across and flicked my nose.

Annoyed, I batted his hand away, but his grin was so contagious, I smiled back anyway. I stuck my tongue out like a two-year-old. "Fine."

Brad rolled his eyes like he was about to reprimand me, but instead of telling me off, he crossed his eyes and stuck out his tongue. "Fine."

I swatted his arm, and he responded by pulling my hair. I shrieked and careened away, checking my wig was still in place. "What, are you eight-years-old?"

"I believe they call it young at heart. This job can make people jaded and humorless, and I don't want that happening to me. You should try it sometime."

I harrumphed, turning onto Albert's street. "I have tried. It didn't work for me."

"Keep trying," said Brad, his voice suddenly serious.

Not knowing how to reply, I quickened my pace. Brad was strangely good at leaving me without words, a trait I found more than a little annoying. We walked the rest of the way in uncomfortable silence.

Albert must have been keeping an eye out because he met us at the door with outstretched arms and a beaming smile. I sank into his hug, reveling in the warmth he offered. He kissed my forehead, hugging me in even closer, oozing love I gobbled up like a starved puppy. I'd missed him far more than I realized. In his arms, I felt like I had a piece of myself back.

Albert pulled Brad in for a hug next, slapping him hard on the back a couple of times. "It's good to see you, son. Thanks for keeping an eye on Lex for me."

Brad stiffened. "It's Milena," he whispered, returning Albert's manly claps. Then louder, "It's not a problem, old man."

I gaped stupidly at the two men, taken back by their obvious affection for each other. I'd never seen Albert show affection toward anyone but Orkney and me. Never.

Feeling uncomfortable, I turned my attention to the new abode, which was less safe house and more warehouse. "So this is … um … nice?" The place was cold, desolate and grimy, nothing like our cozy safe house apartment in Queens. A ratty couch and two chairs were in one corner, a minuscule kitchenette and Formica dining table in another, a folding table with a computer floundered in the expansive middle, and three cots were in the far left corner.

"It was a wool processing warehouse and then an artist

workspace cooperative. The artists put in the kitchenette, and the sofa and chairs are left over from when they were here. I've been sleeping on the couch but ran out and got the cots when Brad said you were coming."

Albert gestured to the sitting area, and we collectively moved in that direction. "Were you Brad's mentor?" I asked, trying to understand the relationship. Brad was covert ops and Albert was an analyst but maybe …

Reaching a chair, I dumped my backpack and collapsed. I was met with a jab from a sprung spring and promptly had to reposition.

"I did some work with the new recruits at The Farm before you came to live with me. Brad was my best student," said Albert, settling into the couch.

Brad shot me a quick glance as he ditched the glasses and pulled out the silicon pouches in his cheeks. The pleasantries over with, it was time to begin good cop, bad cop.

Albert must have caught his glance because he cleared his throat. "Is one of you finally going to fill me in on why you're here? I've been trying to guess since your call, Bradley, but I'm at a loss. It's not a good thing to leave an old man fretting for hours on end, you know?" Albert poured his efforts into what I think was a glare, but his face was far too sweet to be menacing.

I stifled a laugh, but Brad didn't bother, laughing outright. He smiled at me like we were the only two people on earth who got Albert, and perhaps we were. When Albert started to grumble, Brad reigned himself in and turned serious. "M brought in some new intel on the leaders of Perun. We came to take them down and hopefully get the three of you an immunity deal."

"And how did you happen upon such information if you were lying low like I asked?" Albert got up and walked over, his eyes narrowed.

I scrunched back in my seat, shooting Brad a desperate look.

"It doesn't matter—"

Brad's words fell away as Albert tilted my chin, studying my face. He swiped a gentle finger over my bruised jaw, pulling off some of the makeup. He'd been too excited when I first arrived, but now he saw it all, the unevenness caused by the swelling and the slight discoloration despite the makeup. He turned my face side-to-side and pulled up my bangs for a look at my forehead. "What happened?" he asked, voice focused and unflinching. It was a voice that said only the truth would do. Albert continued to look me over, running his hands over my skull, my shoulders, my neck. Feeling the fleabite scabs, he pulled up my hair for a better look.

I slapped his hand away, and he stepped back. I opened my mouth to speak, but nothing came out. I feared his inevitable pitying look. "I ran into my dad," I finally blurted.

I ducked my eyes as Albert's face melted. "How?"

"I was following Amalya, and he grabbed her outside her apartment. I didn't know it was him at first, but when I saw …"

Albert grimaced. "You had to go in."

I nodded. He might not like it, but surely Albert could understand. "I was careful. I had my gun. I was worried about Amalya. He was hurting her."

"How long did you follow her? Did you make contact?" Clearly uncomfortable, Albert's eyes shifted from me to Brad then back again.

"I went to her hotel a couple of times but always in disguise. I was going to stop—"

"Jesus, what were you thinking?" Albert started pacing, shooting darts at me every few seconds. On second thought, maybe Albert could pull off the whole menacing look. "This was exactly why I didn't want to leave you alone and why I called in Brad. I knew you were unraveling. I just knew."

I jumped up. "Unraveling? I'm not—"

"The why of this doesn't matter," said Brad, cutting in. "We've been handed an unbelievable opportunity. You should be thanking M, not yelling at her. M's fine, all things considered. She has it together." Brad nodded to me. "Tell him what you learned."

"Kasarian is one of the leaders of Perun," I said, folding my arms and looking away. "And I think his half-brother, Tarkan Aroyan, could also be a leader. It would explain his unexpected entrance into the Presidential race, his unwillingness to concede defeat and why they kept the whole half-brother thing a secret."

Brad and I spent the next few minutes giving Albert the rundown. "If we can get Kasarian, I think I can work an immunity deal for you, M and Alexandra," said Brad, glancing my way with a reassuring smile.

"Get Kasarian? He's the Goddamn President, and we're three people. One of us is too old, one too young, and one or both of you is clearly delusional. Brad, you're not James Bond." Albert shook his head and gnawed on a thumbnail. "My priority is to extract Alexandra. I'm pulling her at the alternative energy conference in Turkey. Then we're out of here. All of us."

Although he tried to hide it, I could see Brad bristle. As a male covert operative, he probably did think of himself as a bit like James Bond. He certainly looked the part. "We have four people," said Brad. "And one is already in place with Kasarian."

Albert's mouth fell open as he took in Brad's meaning then his head began to shake, slowly at first, then with vehemence.

"No. No. No. That is not happening. Alexandra has been through too much already. It's too dangerous." Albert paced in front of the couch, and every once in a while he mumbled another "no." Brad and I stayed quiet, giving the idea time to percolate.

"Perun trained her Albert; she's not helpless. They messed with her life as much as Milena's. She's going to want to help us. And don't you want to take her home to the States after this is over instead of into hiding?"

"It's true," I chimed in. "Perun broke her. Stole her parents. She's going to want this."

"Not if she doesn't know about it." Albert's fingers twitched nervously. After a few more pacing circuits, he sank into the couch and eyed us with a steely gaze. "I love you both but don't ask me this. She's all that I have left of Gregory. I can't endanger her."

I caught a strange grimace from Brad out of the corner of my eye. "The good of the many outweighs the good of the few. You know that Albert. You drilled it into us at The Farm."

"I'm not with the CIA anymore," spat Albert.

My stomach flopped and roiled at seeing his panic. Albert's normally steady hands shook. Ten minutes before he'd looked like the poster boy for geriatric health. Now he only looked small and frail, the life draining out of him. He was an analyst, not an operative and wasn't used to dealing with this kind of stress.

I got up and went over to hug him. We needed to tread more lightly, maybe give him a break. Brad was winding up for another onslaught, and I shook my head to warn him off, hoping he'd get my meaning. Albert was too old for this sort of thing. As much as I wanted Alexandra's help, I didn't want to give Albert a heart attack to get it. Maybe we didn't need a bad cop. Maybe we needed good cop and mildly pushy cop instead.

Brad ignored me. "We're using Alexandra to get Kasarian. Either you help Milena and me, and we get you guys an immunity deal, or I turn what I know over to the CIA right now, and they'll leverage Alexandra's placement, and the both of you will be left with nothing. One way you win. One way you don't. It's your choice. Alexandra doesn't have one. She'll be helping us regardless."

Shocked at Brad's ultimatum, I squeezed Albert closer, trying to hold him together. He was shaking so hard, and I worried he might come apart at the seams. Now which one of us was unraveling? "If we handle Alexandra, we can help protect her. She's strong, Albert. Really strong. I saw it in her eyes when I met her. She can do this. She'll want to do this to bring herself closure," I said, glaring at Brad. He shrugged as if saying 'it had to be done.'

Albert burst out of my arms without warning. "Fuck you, Brad. How dare you. How dare you put me in this position."

My mouth dropped as Albert stormed away. His panic had shifted to rage lightning fast. Albert went from frail to thundering in a nanosecond. I'd never seen him that angry. I'd also never heard him say *fuck*.

This didn't bode well considering we hadn't even told him about Orkney yet. Ork had helped make us a family. Living a lie had been hard for both Albert and me, and Ork was our wingman. It was Albert's friendship with Ork that helped me see him as something other than a mark, and it was probably the same for him. Ork getting hurt, because I'd been disobedient and followed my grandmother, was only going to piss Albert off further.

Brad's gaze found mine and held. His green eyes stormed.

"What next?" I mouthed.

# FOURTEEN

I NUDGED ALBERT as I plunked a carton of milk and a cereal box onto the kitchen table next to three bowls. "And you worried about me living alone. You've got nothing in your kitchen."

Albert shot me a look but said nothing. I smiled anyway, trying to be Ms. Perky Sunshine. There was only so long Albert could give Brad and me the cold shoulder. I just needed to wait him out. For the last hour, we'd been formulating our plan of attack. Working out the logistics of a plan would help Albert feel more relaxed about Alexandra's situation. At least that was my hope. So far he'd shown no inclination to trade in his pissed off state for something a little more bearable.

"Our best bet is to send M in as a student to share the plan," said Brad. "Alexandra has met M before and is likely to trust her, plus M can pass for a student wanting to chat with a professor. She won't look out of place having an extended conversation."

"She's adjunct faculty and only teaches on Thursday," said Albert, his tone curt. "She has office hours, but the security detail knows her students. There's only twenty."

"M can be a potential student wanting advice. I don't see a problem if we get her the right student ID."

Albert poured cereal into his bowl. "I don't like it. It's too risky for Le—" Albert's voice caught and cereal spilled over the edge of his bowl. "Milena."

"I'll be fine. Perun would never expect me to come to Olissa, and it's the only way to get us the time we need to relay the plan."

Albert threw his hands up. "I see I don't have a say in the matter."

I gave his leg a gentle pat, but Albert grumbled and grabbed his bowl. He ambled to the couch and sat, sending out *stay away from me or else* vibes.

Brad locked eyes with me and scowled, his soulful green eyes pained. He might be willing to pay the price for railroading Albert, but that didn't mean the cold shoulder didn't hurt. With all the *old mans* and *sons,* they tossed around; the two were obviously close. I took Brad's hand, and we sat quietly for a minute, drawing strength from each other. Brad had taken one for the team, and I respected that.

Our silent bonding session ended when my burner buzzed with a call from Martine. "I'll take this over there," I said, gesturing to the far corner with the cots. Three cheers for the privacy of open plan living and a space that echoed.

I retreated to the *bedroom*. "Hey Martine, just one sec." The phone crackled as I jogged, my earring grinding against the receiver. Martine said something I couldn't make out. "One sec. I just need some—" I dove onto my cot and scuttled under the covers. "Privacy. How are you?" In addition to being less than private, the warehouse was also frigid. Brrr.

"It's Grant," said the voice at the other end. "I ran into Martine, and she lent me her burner."

My heart stuttered, shocked to hear Grant's voice. "Where are you?" I blurted. There was a ton of background noise—music, maybe a kid crying, someone shouting. "I ran into Martine at the mall."

"Oh. Okay."

An uncomfortable silence fell between us, and I squeezed my eyes shut. My mouth was thick with a slurry of words I was afraid to say. I'd taken a chance with Grant by coming clean, and when it hadn't worked, I was wrecked. So wrecked I'd had to close the door on him and refuse to feel anything. Now Grant had a crowbar at my door. "What?" I finally said, breaking the silence.

"I … um … well, I wanted to say I'm sorry for how I acted. I was in shock. I couldn't process. Now that I've had time to think …"

Grant's words fell away. A heartbeat passed. Two. Ten. "You what?" I said, unable to stand the heavy void between us. It dug in and twisted like a knife. I felt under attack, my every cell calling for flight. I wanted to retreat and hit the *end* button to save myself. What did I want from him? Forgiveness? A second chance? I could pretend the love of my life hadn't called, couldn't I?

"I'd like the chance to know you. The real you. Maybe then, who knows?"

Now it was my turn to collapse the conversation into silence. Usually, I saw things coming—events, conversations, whatever. I planned my responses. And even if something took me by surprise, I was quick to think on my feet. But now, I had nothing.

"Hey, um, Martine is pulling at my arm. She wants to talk. I'm going to hand the phone over, but please don't hang up until I talk to you again. Okay?"

"Mmmhmm, okay," I whispered. Damn it. What did I

want? Could I trust him? Did I even want to try? What if his dad had told him to get in contact?

"Hey girl," said Martine. "I'm walking away from Grant now, so he can't hear us. I'm sorry for the ambush. I ran into him, and he said he needed to talk with you. I got flustered, and before I knew it, I was handing him my burner."

"It's okay. I get it. So you just ran into him? Did he approach you or did you approach him?"

"He approached me. Why? He looks pitiful M. Pale and pitiful. I don't think he's been eating."

"If he approached you, he might be working for his dad, trying to get information about where I am. I'm going to need to ditch this burner in case he's memorized the number, and you should ditch yours."

"Oh. Shit."

I looked at my watch; I'd been on the phone almost a minute. "I need you to scan your surroundings. Do you see anyone suspicious? Is there anyone with a phone or some sort of tech who stands out? Someone with a Bluetooth ear piece who isn't talking?"

"Oh God. I'm so sorry. I … I … I don't see anyone. At least, I don't think."

"It's fine. I just need to be cautious. When you give the phone back to Grant, I need you to take his phone and any bags he's carrying. Have him empty his pockets. Then I need you to walk away. At least thirty feet. Can you do that?"

"Okay," Martine said, her voice shaky. "I didn't think. I didn't realize. If my opinion's worth anything, I think he's on the level. The boy looks bad. Really sad, you know?"

I sighed. "Okay. Thanks Martine, you can put him back on. Don't forget to ditch the phone after, and I may not be able to get in contact for a while."

"I'm sorry for messing this up. Love you."

"Love you, too."

The phone crackled as Martine returned to Grant. I heard a brief discussion as she relieved him of everything on his person. From the sounds of it, she gave him quite the pat down. When Grant protested as she ran a hand up, what I assume was his thigh, she shot back with "don't get your boxers in a bunch, I'm a lesbian," which made me almost smile.

Martine came back on the line. "He's clear. I was thorough."

"I heard. Thank you."

She handed the phone to Grant, who came back on the line. "Hey."

"Hey," I replied.

"I have a new story to tell you. Want to hear it?" he asked, his voice nervous but hopeful.

"No," I said. "I'm not ready for that. That's too easy for us."

Silence, then "Yeah. I can see that. Sorry. What if we try a couple of phone calls each week? I can get a burner like Martine and call you at designated times."

"I'm a fugitive. I can't schedule things. Besides phones can be tracked."

"Is that why I got a pat down? I'm not trying to track your phone. I wouldn't have the first clue as to how to do that."

"Good to know." He sounded sincere but…

"What about email? We can be pen pals."

"Grant, I appreciate what you're trying to do, but I might always be a fugitive. I'm trying for an immunity deal, but that may never happen. Are you sure you want to go down this road with me? It might not end well."

"I'm willing to take a punt if you are. What's the worst that can happen? We find out we aren't compatible and move on with no *what ifs*."

"Or we find out we're completely and utterly right for each

other, but can never be together because I'm an enemy of the State."

Grant laughed. "Then we lead a tragic life because of our devastating love. Think how romantic that will be."

He laughed, but I could tell he was serious on some level. "Grant, I've had enough tragedy."

"Please, Lex. Let's at least try."

"It's Milena."

Grant laughed nervously. "Yes, of course. Sorry. That will take some getting used to. It's a beautiful name, though. It suits you." My heart skipped a beat, his crowbar gaining leverage. "Give me another chance. Give us another chance. We're worth it."

"Did you tell your dad I came by the house?" I asked, wanting to catch him off guard to see if he might stumble.

He was silent for only a second. "I told him you came by. I'm sorry. I was so mad at you both. I couldn't believe he hadn't told me what you were."

"How do I know you're not trying to help your dad now? Maybe you want me to reveal where I am? You could be baiting a trap."

Grant sucked in a breath so loud I could hear it across the line. "How could you think that? I would never."

"I saw how much you hated me when I told you the truth, and your dad's a persuasive man."

"You lied for over a year, Lex—"

"Milena," I corrected. The more people called me Lex, the more the name gnawed at me. It was a knife cutting skin, each cut deeper than the last. There was an Alexandra Gastone, and I was most definitely not her. I didn't know who I, Milena Rokva, was now, but I desperately wanted to and being called Lex wasn't helping the situation. I needed to leave Lex Gastone in my rearview mirror, and I needed everyone, including Albert and Grant, to leave her there too.

"Why are you trying to make this so hard? Don't you want to give us a chance? I'm sorry about saying the wrong name. I'm sorry I told my dad, but Jesus, I would never help my dad arrest you. You know I loved you. That's gotta count for something." He paused for a beat, letting his words sink in. "You know me."

A crazed laugh bubbled up from deep inside. "I thought I knew my dad until he shot Ork and beat the crap out of me. People lie to themselves," I said, the words dripping off my acid tongue.

A thick, smoggy hush hung heavy on the line. My words had come out in a deluge, my mind unable to dam them. *God damn it. Shut up. Shut up. Shut up.*

"I'm sorry … Milena. I'm so sorry about Ork." Grant's voice cracked. "I don't know what to say. Your life is so … different from mine. I swear you can trust me, though. I'm not lying about myself. I'm the guy you always knew."

There was that word again—trust. Spying was a game of allegiances and trust. Ally with the wrong person and you wouldn't be a spy for long. Instead, you'd be boxed, either in a cell or a coffin. My mind gnawed on the word, turning it over and smacking it around. It flashed red. Danger.

"That crooked smile you liked, was Alexandra's, not mine." There'd been so much hate in his eyes the last time I saw him. At hearing his voice again, that hate slapped me across the cheek and said, "Don't be a silly girl. Don't be a silly spy."

"Show me the real one. I want to know you. The real Milena. For better or worse. There's a good possibility we won't fit together, but there's a chance we will, and I want to take that chance."

"I love ballet, astronomy, and writing. Not cheerleading and math. I would never have been popular."

"I'm a geek, Lex. I don't care about popularity, and you know it. I love football, and it happened to give me social status, but popularity is not something that matters to me. The only perk was finally having a shot with you."

There was truth to his words and they soothed me, but they weren't enough to convince me. Not yet. "You were my mark because of your dad. That's why we got together. It wouldn't have mattered if you were a social outcast. I would have made it work. I would have rebranded myself and sold you to my friends. I wasn't supposed to fall in love with you."

"You're not going to scare me away by being blunt. Whether I was your mark or not, I only care that you loved me."

"Love," I said, my breath catching. "Present tense. I knew who I was falling in love with. You didn't."

"For God's sake, let me find out!"

I thrashed under the covers, adrenaline spiking my system. I ached with the need to run. But should I run toward Grant or away? He'd said all the right things. Pushed all the right buttons. His words rang with sincerity. He'd convinced Martine. All he asked for was a chance. He'd managed to push open my armored door a body width and insert himself. Should I let him through or push him back?

"What if we try the pen pal thing?" offered Grant. "You can bounce the email off different servers around the world, so it's untrackable. You can protect yourself."

"You been marathoning spy movies?"

Grant laughed. "I can neither verify nor deny that assertion. Although I must say *The Americans* pretty much rocked my world and John Le Carré and Olen Steinhauer are both the Man."

"That so?"

"Oh God, yes! Hey, maybe you'll write your story someday

after it's all over."

"Never gonna happen."

"Never say never. So what's it going to be? Are we going to try this?"

# FIFTEEN

TWO DAYS LATER—mission day—I walked over to the warehouse window under the guise of getting a better look at my new student ID. "Looks legit," I said, twisting it in the light. It had the same holographic university seal I'd seen in the pictures online. I glanced at my watch and tapped my fingers on the window. *Come on. Come on. Come on.*

Varos was due any minute. I'd contacted him back in the States as soon as Brad green-lighted my idea. If this mission was going to go down the way I wanted it to, with the other cadets protected, I needed Varos' help, despite his questionable mental health. He was the best tech guy I knew.

Brad laughed, stomping on the backpack we'd just purchased as part of my disguise. "It looks legit because it is. My guy knows someone in the registrar's office."

And there he was, our special guest to this little coup attempt. He ambled toward the warehouse, in no hurry whatsoever. Jeez. I walked to the door. "So Albert, Brad, I want to tell you something." I felt like a shitheel springing Varos on them at the last minute, but if I'd been polite and asked first, Brad and Albert wouldn't have allowed it. Varos was a wild card variable they wouldn't want to deal with. We each had our agenda and while taking down Kasarian was on everyone's to-do list, protecting the other cadets was only on mine, and I needed Varos to do that.

Albert and Brad looked my way, left eyebrows arched. "Hmmm?" they said in unison, their bodies tensing slightly.

"I know you're not going to like it, but it's too late, so you're just going to have to deal. I—"

Brad hurried to the window. "M, what did you do?"

Albert ran a nervous hand through his hair. "You didn't?"

"What did she do?" asked Brad.

"We need help—a tech person. So I called in my friend Varos." I opened the door as Varos stepped up to knock. "Come on in," I said. I smiled while surreptitiously evaluating Varos for any signs of the crazy. Nothing jumped out as off, but then again it hadn't last time either. "We've been waiting for you."

Varos shrugged off his bag then picked me up in a giant, bone-crushing bear hug. With lightning fast reflexes, Brad was by my side, waiting to take out Varos if I needed. "It's fine," I croaked.

"I'm so glad you came to your senses," Varos said, planting a kiss on one cheek then the other. He started to go for another kiss, this time to the mouth, but thought better of it, depositing me back on my feet where I greedily gobbled air. Varos gestured to the room with a frown. "Nice Batcave, although I can't say I'm thrilled with the company you're keeping."

"Likewise," said Albert, marching over and grabbing my arm. "Milena, we need to talk." I signed one minute to Varos and stumbled after Albert as he not so gently tugged me away. "What were you thinking?" he spat. If he whispered our conversation might have been private, but Albert was in no mood for decorum. He might as well have been talking with a megaphone.

"I thought we needed more hands on deck. If Alexandra's going to get the goods on Kasarian, we need to get safely into his computer network without being detected. Varos has the hardware for that. He knows more about the protocols, firewalls, and system safety nets than anyone else. Having him on our side will help keep Alexandra safe. We want to get this done and dusted before extracting her at the energy conference don't we?"

Albert's face jogged through a range of emotions as he thought things over. There was some rapid blinking, grimacing, deep breathing and finally a sound emanating from deep within impossible to properly characterize—a grumbling sort of growly groan if such a thing exists. "Fine, but I'm going to watch him like a hawk." Albert raised his voice and pointed at Varos. "Like a hawk."

Varos smirked, raising his hand in salute.

I shot Varos a death glare before glancing Brad's way, wondering how he was dealing with my curve ball.

As if reading my mind, Brad held out his hand. "Bradley Thomas, CIA," he said. "Nice to meet you. Any friend of M is a friend of mine."

Varos narrowed his eyes, probably wondering if Brad was serious. The CIA was no doubt in a dead heat with Perun on his list of groups not to trust. Varos flicked his eyes my way, and I nodded my encouragement. "Nice to meet you too," he managed to mumble. "Name's Varos."

"You bring what I need?" I asked.

"Yep," said Varos, pulling a memory stick and smartphone from his jacket pocket. "Once she's inserted the stick into his computer, it will take about a minute to download my worm into Kasarian's system. His phone will have more encryption so mirroring that may take ten minutes or more."

Brad snaked a hand through his hair in dismay. "We already have our versions of this stuff ready to go."

"Not this good. Even you admitted we only had a 50/50 shot of being able to crack his phone with our tech. If we're going to ask Alexandra to do this, we need to get everything we can. Trust me."

"Let me take a look at it," said Brad, nodding for me to follow.

Varos pointed to the side of the warehouse opposite where Brad, Albert and I had our beds. "I'll go pitch my sleeping bag over there."

Apparently being one big, happy Perun-hating family was not in the cards. Not that I expected as much, but a girl can dream.

I must have been moving too slow for Brad because he reached back and grabbed my wrist, jerking me forward. "What?" I said, annoyed.

"I don't like surprises. Especially not right before we green-light a mission. You're leaving in half an hour to meet Alexandra."

"We need him. I'm serious about his tech. It's top notch. No one does it better. And more importantly, I need him here. I want someone whose only allegiance is to me. Albert loves me, but he's also got Alexandra to think about. You've got the CIA. I need someone watching my back."

Brad paused midstride and turned. He opened his mouth then clamped it shut a second later, his lips twisting grimly, the muscles in his jaw twitching. His eyes found mine and his fingers slid into my hand. His thumb absently stroked my palm. We stayed that way for several heartbeats, me unblinking while Brad's turbulent eyes fought to say what he could not. Something was keeping me from reading his eyes as my heart revved wildly. I think it was fear. I ducked my eyes and slid my hand away. I didn't know Brad. Not enough, anyway. The old, 'any friend of Albert is a friend of mine,' didn't work for me. "I have your back, M. I swear," whispered Brad, tucking a hand under my chin and raising my gaze.

I stared wide-eyed, trying to find the lie in his words. When I couldn't, I squeezed my eyes shut and sucked in a breath. "Good to know. Thank you."

A good guy, Brad would have my back until he couldn't anymore, and I was thankful for whatever caused his loyalty, be it his relationship with Albert or any brotherly fondness he'd developed after surveilling me for so many years. That said, if push came to shove, I knew he'd choose the CIA over me, which was fair enough. His allegiance should be to his country. I couldn't rightfully expect anything else.

Varos and I would watch each other's backs while also watching the backs of the other Perun cadets. The CIA could have Perun, but if Varos or I had any say in the matter, they would not have the locations and cover identities of our friends. People like Isra could keep their new identities or leave them, but it would be their choice.

# SIXTEEN

IT POURED RAIN as I sprinted toward Voskova Hall, where Alexandra had her visiting lecturer's office. She was currently teaching her class, but had office hours directly after, and I wanted to be the first in line. I had on a red wig, my scholarly glasses, and a neat but unmemorable ensemble of jeans, rain boots and a local brand of Gore-Tex rain jacket. I looked like every other Olissan student dashing through the pelting rain. No one bothered with an umbrella because the wind would turn one inside out within seconds. It was best to run as fast as you could and hope for the best. My newly purchased and recently distressed backpack—complete with a few dirt smudges and stray pen marks—bobbed up and down on my back as I ran, a chemistry and advanced calculus book inside for legitimacy along with a spy thriller by Le Carré. If Alexandra's bodyguards were worth their salt, they'd search me, and I needed to be every inch the student.

We appropriately aged both textbooks giving them torn pages and tons of highlighting and the spy thriller … well, that was reverse psychology. In addition to my books, the backpack had my wallet, a half pack of gum, pens and pencils, stray receipts, paper scraps and lint. Legitimately plausible accessories were a spy's best friend, and could make anyone wary about your identity doubt themselves just enough for you to scrape by.

Entering Voskova, I shook off the rain and shrugged off my coat as I turned left down the main hall headed for the stairs. I'd studied the building schematic for my escape routes as well as to avoid looking like a newbie. *I was a student here, yes I was.* Alexandra's office was up four flights of stairs, which I took at a leisurely pace as I dug out my phone. I didn't spot any cameras in the stairwell, and the chances were good there weren't any, but just in case, I continued to play my part as a student, humming the tune of an Olissan pop song and reading a text from my *boyfriend.*

Varos: I think of our kiss in the park every day … run away with me.

I paused midstride. What the hell? I was expecting a text from Varos; it was part of my cover but not this.

Me: Are you kidding?

Varos: No. I'm entirely serious. Come away with me. I've got the perfect place picked. Beaches. Fruity drinks.

Me: Now is not the time for this!!!!!

Varos: Did I mention fruity drinks?

Me: You're a jerk. Goodbye.

Varos hadn't seemed crazy, but clearly he still was. *Damn him.*

I was on a mission. Everything else could wait. Varos could be dealt with later. Much later. Maybe never. God. He was such a jerk. A stupid, crazy jerk. Mounting the last flight of stairs, I angrily shook away thoughts of him. At the door, I squared my shoulders and took a breath relinquishing any thoughts of Varos.

*Ready or not, here I come.*

Alexandra's office was down the hall. I couldn't miss it, what with the official looking black suited He-Man stationed out front. If his suit and grim demeanor didn't give away his purpose, the telltale spiral comms cord snaking down from his ear certainly did. The university must really want Alexandra on staff—probably because of her high visibility—to put up with the extra security measures. Big, burly men in black, definitely did not scream higher academia. I gave the guard a wary, side-eyed appraisal like any normal student before plopping down by the door and pulling out a book and some gum. *No reason to look at me. I'm just your normal college girl. Yes, sirree.*

I wasn't halfway through the Le Carré novel I'd purchased the day before, and already I could see why Grant enjoyed Le Carré. Reading about spies was loads more fun than being one. Maybe I should have been reading espionage thrillers all along. Perhaps I'd have thought my life was super cool instead of a soul-sucking drag.

I'd chosen to take the leap with Grant and now found myself prepping for the email I planned to send that night. If Grant was mainlining spy fiction, I wanted to know what he was picking up, true and untrue. Plus, we'd always talked about books, movies, and TV, so it gave us a comfortable jumping off point.

Unable to concentrate on reading with the guard looming, I contented myself to flick a page every minute or so and blow some bubbles. Instead of feet away, it felt like the guard was only inches, with his loud Vaderesque breathing. Finally, the elevator at the end of the hall pinged open, and Alexandra wheeled out, flanked by three more security guards. I popped up and brushed off my backside.

Alexandra was as I remembered. Her body was small and broken while her eyes, at least the one real one, was sharp. Alive. Ferocious. "Dr. Kasarian, I was hoping to talk to you for a minute." I stepped forward with my hand out, but Vader stepped in front of me.

"ID please," he said, holding a hand out. Playing my role, I jumped back with a yelp.

"Um, okay," I said, reaching down for my bag and wallet. "I wanted to talk with Dr. Kasarian about her seminar next semester. I don't have all the prerequisites but really want to take it."

"Lenko, I'm sure she's fine. Do we have to do this every time?" said Alexandra, wheeling out from behind him.

"Yes. Ms. Kasarian we do. You know that," grumbled Lenko, eyeballing my ID. He produced a smartphone with scanner attachment and slid the ID through.

It took Alexandra all of two seconds to recognize me. Her eyes went wide for a half-second before she recovered. Fortunately, the guards were focused on me and didn't notice. I smiled, hoping to provide reassurance. Her lips spread into a grim line, and I wondered if it was the surprise of being contacted or the fact I was doing the contacting that was making her unhappy.

I'd felt a closeness to her at the gala, and I'd have bet she felt the same, but now that time had passed, I wouldn't be surprised if she'd grown to hate my guts. I'd lived her life, after all. My existence was part of the reason she was in a wheelchair, and her parents were dead. On my end, I felt less connected than I had.

We'd shared a rare moment of surprised realization and camaraderie at being stuck in such an odd situation. Now, though, if I was totally honest, I couldn't help but see her as a threat to my relationship with Albert. If Albert had to choose between us, he would choose Alexandra. If Alexandra wanted me gone, I would be. The worst part was, I couldn't blame her. She'd have to be a saint to want me sticking around in her life.

Lenko's brow furrowed as he waited for my ID to come up in the system. I tried to look unworried as I waited.

And waited.

And waited.

My heartbeat kicked up a notch.

Good God, had the *friend* in the registrar's office messed things up somehow?

I sighed and put a hand on my hip. "What's the hold-up?" I asked, my muscles coiling tight. There was an exit twenty feet behind me that was my plan B if things went bad. Stationed in the lobby, Brad was ready to help if needed. All I'd have to do was make it down the stairwell.

"It's thinking," said Lenko. He signaled to one of the security detail. "Check her bag."

"Wait, what?" I asked, clutching my bag and looking worried.

"Standard protocol," said the guard, gesturing for me to hand it over.

"But that's an invasion of privacy."

"You got some dirty knickers in there?" the guard asked, his smile wicked.

"No!" Students crowded the hall, and I could tell this perv

would love to shame me by waving a pair of panties around.

"Maybe some weed?" he asked, snatching the bag. I grabbed for it but missed on purpose. *What was taking so long with that ID?* A couple of students walking by caught my eye and gave me a pained *I feel for you* look. I nodded and rolled my eyes.

Growing tired of the pitying looks from the other students, I chanced a glance at Alexandra. Her eyes blinked madly, and her mouth twitched at intervals, her eyes darting from me to Lenko and back again. She was not as skilled at hiding her emotions as I'd hoped. She looked about ready to bolt from her wheelchair.

The goon with my bag opened it and shuffled items around. He pulled out both textbooks and flicked through them and made several stunning yuck faces as he dug around in the scraps at the bottom. I may or may not have had a few wrapped up pieces of soggy chewing gum down there. "Bag's clear," he said, offering it back.

I snatched it and slung it over my shoulder. "You done yet?" I asked Lenko. *Come on, come on, come on.* I leaned in to look at the scanner just as it pinged, my ID photo popping onto the screen. Lenko scrolled through my profile, probably looking for journalism courses (it wouldn't do for a wannabe Woodward or Bernstein to get an unplanned quote from Vladik Kasarian's sister) or involvement in political groups. When nothing but chem and math classes showed up, he waved Alexandra into her office and handed me back my card. "We'll need to pat you down and take your phone."

I rolled my eyes again. "Don't get nosy," I said, handing my phone to one guard while putting my legs and arms out wide for the pat down.

"You talking about the phone or the body search?" said the guard, running a hand under my boobs. It was standard pat down procedure, but I flinched anyway and glared. "Perv much?"

"She's clear," he said, herding me not so gently into the office.

Phase one complete.

"Please, shut the door, Lenko," said Alexandra. "I've got a headache and can't take all that noise out there." She waved her hand at the students in the hall.

Lenko nodded. "Yes, ma'am."

I took a seat opposite Alexandra and smiled, wanting to put her at ease. We didn't speak until the door clicked closed. "Thanks for seeing me Dr. Kasarian," I said, pointing to my ear and gesturing to the room at large.

"Did something happen? Is everything okay with my grandfather?" Alexandra waved dismissively at the room. "It's clear. You can speak freely."

"Albert's fine but an opportunity has presented itself, and we need your help."

Alexandra leaned in, folding her hands on the desk. Her eyes studied me, taking in every inch of who I was on the surface then probing deeper for more. Everything about her was impassive except her eyes. They were scalpels, peeling away my flesh for what lay beyond the veneer. They searched for something, but what, I didn't know. Was it penance she wanted to see? Loyalty to Albert and to her? Or was it just my competence she wanted to establish? She was a genius, and I was her intellectual peon, maybe she worried I didn't have what it took to be in her league. Gone was the shaken girl from the gala. Alexandra might be worried about Albert, but she was still playing the spy game to the best of her ability, trying to scope out my intentions. Her demeanor was uncomfortably cold. Gal pals, we were not, at least not yet. For both the mission and my long-term happiness, I hoped to change that.

I cleared my throat and smiled. When she pulled her eyes back to mine, I leaned forward mirroring her position, a subconscious means of putting her at ease. "Recent evidence indicates Vladik Kasarian is one of Perun's leaders and his brother Tarkan Aroyan may be as well."

I paused to let her digest the revelation, expecting her to be shocked. But nope, she didn't miss a beat, instead laughing, a strangled sort of barking laugh. "That's impossible. I would know." She shook her head. "If Vladik is Perun, why place me with him? It makes no sense."

"It makes perfect sense if Perun is fissuring. We think the brothers are at war. That's why Tarkan entered the Presidential race. He wanted to stop his brother's power grab. Vladik took you to keep your genius for himself."

"Brothers? What are you talking about?" Alexandra's voice arced higher and higher. "Vladik has no brothers."

"Keep your voice down," I said calmly, trying to steady her. "A CIA analysis of their blood revealed Vladik and Tarkan are half-brothers."

Alexandra eyeballed me like I had three heads. "No, it's not possible. There's some mistake. I would know if he had a brother." Her hands balled into white-knuckled fists. "Trust me. I would know. We're very close."

As smart as Alexandra was, I was shocked to find she remained naïve to the ways of the spy game. I reached across the table for her hands, but she jerked them away. "You're a pawn, just like I was," I said, locking eyes. Hers were wild. Uncertain. "You're a means to an end. They told you what you needed to know. He took you for himself because he wants your genius. Perun has infiltrated the world energy markets, and once your research on cold fusion is complete, Vladik will collapse the markets and take hold of the world's energy supply. Nations around the world will be beholden to Olissa."

"You're saying he let me pretend to be his sister, even though he knew who I was all along? That's ridiculous. I have a handler. I gather intel."

"They were giving you what you needed to believe the farce. It's ingenious. Anonymity is power."

Alexandra dropped her eyes and spun toward the window. I said nothing, letting her have a moment to think. I hated not being able to see her face. The tiniest little facial movements can give away so much, a little tic in the mouth indicates nervousness, a narrowing of the eyes hints at anger, a tightening of the throat suggests the person is fighting tears. With Alexandra, I was privy to none of the usual cues. She was stock still in her chair. Stone. I was left watching the clock. Tick tock, tick tock.

"We need your help," I said again, breaking the silence after a minute. Although I understood her shock, I could only give her so long to contemplate. I opened my bag and pulled out my keys. Hidden in a mini Rubik's Cube keychain was a thumb drive. I dislodged it and set it on the desk. I pulled the phone from its hidden compartment underneath the lint and gum wrappers and set it alongside. Alexandra finally turned around. Her face was unreadable, a chiseled piece of granite giving nothing away. I wanted to see anger and frustration in her eyes. I wanted her to be so mad she'd jump at the chance to help. Now, all I could do was hope she was feeling it but had buried it deep. I pointed to the phone. "We need you to mirror his phone with this. His phone will have encryption so it may take a while. Only do it when you have plenty of time—ten minutes or more."

"And the thumb drive?" she asked, picking it up.

"We need you to plug it into both his personal and office

computers. We don't know how he's pulling the strings within Perun, so we want to cover our bases. The drive contains a worm that will allow us access to his systems. The upload should only take a few minutes."

Alexandra picked up the phone and held both devices, studying them. She was infuriatingly mute. She was not responding how I'd expected.

"I know it's a lot to take in, Alexandra. I know—" she flinched, and I stopped abruptly, wondering what was wrong. Then I realized, I'd said her real name. A name she hadn't been called in years. "Alexandra," I said again, letting the name roll off my tongue slowly. I wanted her to hear it. To take it in. She was not Alina Kasarian. She was Alexandra Gastone. Perun killed her parents and stole her life. She might be a genius, but she was still a pawn in their game, just like me, just like the rest of the cadets. "We need you to help us right this wrong. You're in a perfect position, posing as his sister. The danger will be minimal and the rewards huge."

Her eyes flicked from the devices to me. "There are always two sides to every story," she said, blinking.

"What?" I asked, confused.

Alexandra set the devices down and reached out a hand. It jarred me to find her face suddenly inviting, but I let her take my hand. She clasped it and squeezed tight. "My research will change the world. It can fix everything."

I shook my head. "It depends on whose hands it's in whether your research will save or kill. In Perun's hands, it could destroy the world if they collapse the energy markets. People will freeze. Starve."

"Whose hands?" asked Alexandra, her face puzzled. "I'm …" she shook her head. "Vladik is a good man. He wants to save the world. And Perun has been behind my research. They're not all bad. They helped me realize my potential.

They pushed me to achieve and to become something special! I think you forget what they gave you."

"They murdered your parents," I blurted. "How can you—"

"I'm not saying Perun is wholly good. They are … flawed. But your view is too narrow. You only see the black and white. The bad. I know Vladik. I know he's good. And think about all that's been done to your country. How can you turn your back on Olissa now?"

I stared at her. *What the fuck?* "You're not Olissan. You're American. Your country will suffer. Your people."

Alexandra shook her head. "America's time has been and gone. It's a decaying giant."

I pulled my hand away. "You told Albert you were willing to be extracted. That you wanted to go home with him."

Alexandra sat back in her chair. "And I do. He's my family. My research into cold fusion is almost done. I'll be presenting it at the energy conference in Istanbul. After that, I can walk away. Olissa can have my research, and I can have my life."

"What if you're wrong about Vladik? Your research will be—" My words fell away as the office lights flicked off along with the heating system. Even though there were no tactical reasons for Alexandra's guards to sabotage the electrical systems if they'd found me out, my adrenaline surged. Alexandra, on the other hand, was the picture of relaxation.

"Don't worry. It's just a quick blackout. They happen all the time," she said, smiling. As if on cue, the lights flicked back on. "See, no need to worry." Her smile broadened. "Once cold fusion is out in the world; blackouts will be a thing of the past."

"I can't help but worry. If you're wrong about Vladik, your research can be used to cripple whole nations."

She shook her head. "You don't know Vladik as I do. He wants the world to be a better place, and my research can help make that a reality. He wants a world with enough energy for everyone, from the poorest countries to the richest. If Perun has fissured, it's because he's trying to protect that dream."

"You're deluding yourself."

Her mouth twisted into an ugly sneer. "I'm a genius. You're the one who's deluded. You know nothing."

Taken back, I fought to control my anger. I told myself people in shock sling words they don't mean. I took a breath striving for calm. Both of us flying off the handle would not lead to anywhere I wanted to go. I nodded to the phone and thumb drive. "There's only one way to find out which one of us is right. I'd love for Vladik to be the man you think he is. I want my country to have a good leader, but what if he's not? Don't we owe it to the world to find out? I know you must blame me for all that happened. For stealing your life. But please don't let that blind you. You owe it to yourself to find out the truth. That's all I'm asking. The phone will allow you to see everything we're seeing. He lied to you about his brother; he could easily be lying about his endgame."

I sucked in a breath. Having played good cop, I now needed to play bad. Or if not bad, at least blunt. "If you don't help us, and you're wrong about Vladik, everything that happens—the chaos, the death—it will all be on you. Do you want that? Are you willing to take the risk? Albert might never forgive you if you're wrong."

Alexandra's eyes narrowed, and her jaw muscles tightened. If looks could kill, I would have taken my last breath. A veil fell as she gathered her composure. "I don't hate you. What happened wasn't your fault."

"I'm glad you feel that way."

"What if Vladik's not guilty?" asked Alexandra, her mouth a hard, unwavering line. Despite her intensity, I didn't look away. I might not be her intellectual equal, but I could damn well play the spy game better. "I will have given the US an all-access pass to the inner workings of the Olissan government and her President. I'm not okay with that."

"I'm not okay with it either. I know I'm asking a lot, but I need you to trust me. I have another cadet working with me. We will make sure the US doesn't get their hands on anything they shouldn't. We're going to protect the other cadets, and if Vladik is the man you say he is, we'll protect him too. Our loyalty, first and foremost, is to Olissa. I've given up my life and my family for this country; I'm not going to betray her now."

"How do I know you're not a liar?"

Someone knocked on the office door as I opened my mouth. The handle turned, and Lenko stuck his head in. "You've got two other students waiting to see you and a meeting across town at two."

Alexandra smiled. "Thank you. We'll be done in a minute."

Lenko nodded and closed the door.

"How do I know you're not a liar?"

I zipped my backpack and stood. "I told Albert about you; that's how. I love him more than you could know, and I could have kept him for myself, but I didn't. After everything, I felt like I owed both of you a chance to know each other, no matter the cost to me." I leaned forward, tapping the phone, "I trust you'll use these, and I look forward to seeing you at the extraction. Albert can't wait to meet you." At the door, I turned back. One more thing needed saying. "Albert devoted his life to avenging your death. He knew I wasn't you from the beginning but said nothing, hoping to one day turn me. He deserves to see you again. Please don't let him down."

I opened the door and left, snagging my phone from Lenko with a sweet smile. "Have a nice day," I sang as I walked away.

I wasn't 100 percent sure I had Alexandra on the hook, but hoped like hell I'd done enough. I'd appealed to her reason, her heart, and her fear. It was a triple threat combo that would work on most people. Alexandra was difficult to read, though. I wondered if her high IQ was making it hard for her to believe Perun had duped her. At the gala, I hadn't read her as arrogant, but now I wasn't so sure. I didn't expect our encounter to be a hugs and puppies affair, but I also didn't expect her to defend Perun. No, our encounter had gone very differently than I'd envisioned. She was not the same woman I'd met. She seemed far less … fragile, and while I had sufficient distance from Perun for their indoctrination efforts to mellow over the years, Alexandra had not. I should have foreseen her reluctance, but my hatred of Perun blinded me to their allure. For each cadet, they found what fueled us and preyed upon it. For me, it was wanting to avenge my mother's death. For Alexandra, it would have been something else, something tailor-made to garner her loyalty. But what?

# SEVENTEEN

LEFT TO WAIT and hope for Alexandra to infiltrate Vladik's network with the worms I'd given her, I decided to work on improving the relationships at home, especially between Brad and Albert. So I'd picked up the makings for a special dinner. Living under the same roof with three men barely speaking was beginning to grate. The atmosphere was palpably tense, and I hoped—no, prayed—a traditional Olissan celebration meal with a roast, fried potato dumplings, and lemon pie might ease tensions and get people talking. Going for broke, I'd also picked up some vodka and beer to help loosen lips.

Setting the bowl with the potato dumplings on the table, I sat down and smiled, "Bon appétit!"

"Looks good. Thanks." Brad grabbed a serving spoon.

"Yep, thanks," said Varos.

Albert gave me a nod and a half smile, which looked like it came with great effort.

"So, how was everyone's day?" I asked.

"Fine," said Brad and Varos, each dumping heaping spoonfuls on their plates.

Albert shrugged.

My stomach dipped. Clearly I needed to work on my phrasing, maybe leave my questions more open-ended to spark something other than monosyllabic replies. I took a bite of the roast, giving myself time to think and found the meat tough. Yuck. I looked around to see if everyone else was finding it tough, and saw Brad and Varos scarfing theirs down like they couldn't get away from the table fast enough.

I quickly swallowed my lump of roast. I needed to engage the group before they fled. "More vodka?" I asked, holding up the bottle.

Brad and Varos nudged their glasses my way.

"I hope you're not planning on pouring yourself a glass," said Albert.

I poured the vodka first into Varos' glass then Brad's. "You know Olissans routinely let their children have vodka. It's practically the national drink. My mom—"

Albert cut me off with a glare, and I promptly shut up. I waggled the bottle at him and nodded, asking if he wanted some.

Albert shook his head.

"Come on, old man. M's eighteen. You bought her a gun for her birthday, but you're not willing to let her drink?" asked Brad.

While Brad chided Albert, Varos shot me a *what the hell* look. "It's not like he's your real grandfather and you have to listen," whispered Varos, nodding at Albert as he stuffed in a gigantic bite of pie. His eyes immediately went wide as his face puckered. He swallowed it down, but it looked to be a close call.

"Now's not the time for Lex to be experimenting with alcohol. She has enough on her plate," said Albert. Turning to Varos, "She *is* my granddaughter. I raised her, and you can kindly remember that. My opinion matters. Doesn't it?" he asked, turning to me.

I nodded and gave Albert a small smile before glancing at Varos and Brad, wishing they would read my mind and get off this topic.

"Her name's Milena," said Varos, rolling his eyes. "Why can't you get that right, Gastone? M-i-l-e-n-a R-o-k-v-a. Not Lex. She's not your granddaughter. She's Olissan."

I kicked Varos under the table. So much for pleasant conversation.

"You need to shut the hell up," said Brad.

Albert stood. "Son, that's the first thing you've said all week I agree with." Albert grabbed his plate and deposited it in the kitchen, leaving me alone with Varos and Brad.

I'd started the dinner wanting everyone to talk, and now all I wanted was to finish as fast as possible. I forked a potato dumpling and shoved it into my mouth.

"You overstepped," said Brad, pointing his fork at Varos.

Varos cocked his head and smiled. "I. Don't. Care."

Brad rolled his eyes.

After two hours of cooking, dinner lasted seven minutes and twelve seconds. To add insult to injury, the potato dumplings were the only dish that tasted passably good. The pie was so tart it was downright inedible. I shoved in my last bite of potato and stood. "Someone else can clean up. Sorry, it sucked. No, wait, I'm not sorry. Sucky people deserve sucky food." I turned on my heels and retreated to *the bedroom* area of the warehouse. What I wouldn't give for some walls.

Varos laughed while Brad called, "Sorry, M." Nearby at our computer station, Albert didn't say anything, but I expected a heartfelt conversation about my *sucky people* comment later. I couldn't wait.

Tucking myself under my cot blanket, I opened my laptop.

I'd been putting off checking my email, conflicted about whether I wanted Grant to have written or bailed on the pen pal idea. After the dinner from hell, I figured either option was fine. My stomach flip-flopped as I opened my account. I held my breath and tapped the inbox key. To keep our conversations as secure as possible, I'd set both Grant and I up with alternate email addresses, and as he'd suggested, I was bouncing my email off a slew of different servers to keep my location secure.

My inbox popped up with one unread message titled 'Agent 00 Requesting Contact.' I smiled and clicked. Grant couldn't get any more adorably dorky.

Dear She Who Must Not Be Named,

I've started this email so many times only to delete everything after a line or two. I have so much to say, but I don't know how to start.

I miss you. Every day I forget you're gone and expect to see you at school. Our friends have been asking about you. I told them you have a sick aunt. Hope that's okay? I didn't think you'd want them to know about rehab or the whole highly trained covert operative thing.

Okay, writing this email is way tougher than I imagined. I've got less than fifty words and it's been an hour. It's funny because you used to be so easy to talk to. I guess that's the problem. You're not you anymore. You're not Lex, and I don't know Milena yet.

I have so many questions but can't seem to weave

them into anything approaching the witty email I imagined writing you. I guess all there is to do is ask the questions. To go completely OCD nerd on you, I'm even going to number them. I'll start easy ...

1. What's your favorite color? (Easy, right?)

2. Star Wars or Star Trek? (There's only one correct answer to this by the way)

3. Favorite book?

4. Why do you love ballet?

5. What's the best part about being a spy?

6. What's the worst?

7. Could you kill me with your bare hands? (Be honest, no delusions of grandeur)

8. What do you like about me?

9. What was your favorite moment of us together?

10. Try to frighten me away. Tell me your darkest secret.

I have a million more questions, but I'll keep it to ten. Sorry for not being more eloquent and just throwing these at you.

I'm crossing my fingers you'll write back. If not, please

know we did have something, and it wasn't all a lie. I realize that now. I realize how hard living as Alexandra must have been and that you were working for a cause. You asked me to forgive you, and for what it's worth, I do.

Agent 00

A tightness, I didn't realize I held, released when I reached the end of the email. Not only had Grant not asked any questions suggesting he was his dad's lackey, but he'd forgiven me. I had it in writing. He forgave me, Milena Rokva—a girl he didn't yet know but wanted to. I'd lied about almost everything including my identity, and he forgave me. I was absolved. Liberated. Gravity's force had lightened.

I hit the reply button and dove into Grant's questions. For better or worse, the boy I loved was finally going to meet the real me.

Dear Agent 00,

I miss you too! And I'm glad you wrote. I was so nervous bringing up my email. I thought maybe you'd have changed your mind.

So, Agent 00, I have a sick Aunt, do I? LOL. Works for me! I appreciate you trying to keep my integrity intact. And to the questions …

1. My favorite color is turquoise, like the color of the Caribbean ocean. I've never seen water that color in person, but I want to.

2. Star Wars but only episodes four through seven. Han Solo and Rey rock and Jar Jar Binks should not exist.

3. *The Fountainhead.* I like how free-thinking and independent Howard Roark is.

4. I love ballet because it's art through movement. It's strength, grace, and beauty all rolled into one. It's art that we need our whole physical body and mind to create. Writing and painting only need our hands, arms, and eyes, but ballet needs all of us. It needs us to be both physically and mentally strong.

5. The best part of being a spy? My immediate response is nothing. Upon further consideration, though, I guess the best part is believing in a cause so worthy it drives you and gives your life meaning. You have something so important to you that you're willing to both live and die for the cause. There's a surprising amount of peace that comes from holding a cause so close to your heart.

6. The worst part? Spying is lying, hiding and lying some more. It's not fun, or at least it never was for me.

7. In all honesty, yes, I could kill you with my bare hands. Do you find that sexy? Mortifying?

8. I love everything about you. I love that you're smart, kind, athletic, geeky. I love that you love photography. I love that you're punctual when our friends make a game of being late. I love that you're romantic, and I

love how your efforts at being romantic sometimes fail. I love how you see the world. I loved watching you with Ork, and I loved watching you watching me. I love your lips, your dimples, your beautiful eyes peering at me from behind your glasses. I love all of it.

9. My favorite moment? God that's hard. I don't think there's only one. Every time I lost myself in one of your kisses, I connected with you in a way I hadn't with anyone else, not even Albert. I was more me in those moments than in any other. I was letting myself love, letting myself connect in ways I'd guarded against.

10. You want me to scare you away, huh? Okay, here's my best shot. Last time I saw my father, I tried to kill him.

So, did I scare you? Are you ready to run away screaming?
Turnabout is fair play. I have a few questions for you …

1. The poem on the back of my picture, tell me why you wrote those words? Tell me what they mean?

2. What scares you the most about me?

3. I've started reading spy books, can you recommend a good one?

I hope you write back, but if not, I understand. I'm glad you wanted to give us a chance.

She Who Must Not Be Named

# EIGHTEEN

THE SOUND OF Brad and Varos bickering wrenched me from sleep. I looked at my watch. It was five freaking a.m. God, I hated living in an echo chamber. Figuring my likelihood of getting back to sleep was nil, and I should probably check on the boys, I rubbed the sleep from my eyes and stretched. My back twinged like an old granny, and I moaned, retreating into a fetal ball. My cot was saggy, and my pampered body was used to a thick, pillow top mattress I could melt into like a cloud. After a momentary pity party, I rolled out of bed, wrapping myself in the wool blanket. It was so cold I could see my breath. Nearby, Albert slept fitfully, no doubt because of the noise. I kissed his forehead then weaved my way over to Brad and Varos.

"Anything yet from Alexandra?" I asked, not caring about interrupting. From what I could tell they were talking about the oh so important topic of Brad drinking out of the milk jug.

"It's still disgusting," said Varos.

Brad glared at Varos. "It was my milk. I drink skim. The regular milk is for everyone else." Brad looked at me for help.

"M, tell him. I wasn't rude; it was *my* milk."

"How old are you?" asked Varos, rolling his eyes.

"He's 28," said Albert coming up behind and biffing Brad on the head. "Varos is right, son. Drinking out of the jug is disgusting."

"Yes!" said Varos, holding a hand up in victory. "Vindicated by the old man. Thank you."

I shot Varos a look at his *old man* comment, but it flew over his head. Whoosh.

"If we're all going to live together we need to be considerate," continued Albert. "Like keeping our voices down when others are sleeping and being thoughtful with food and drinks."

Brad threw up his hands with a huff. "It was *my* milk."

Albert skirted around the table to take a look at the computers. "Anything from Alexandra?"

I nudged Brad with my elbow. "I get it. It was your milk," I whispered with a smile.

He nudged me back then wrapped an arm around my shoulder. "I know, right? Some people." He shook his head, narrowing his eyes at Varos.

"Nothing yet," said Varos, his eyes locking on Brad's arm.

"Hmmm," said Albert, one side of his mouth folding down into a half-frown. "Hope everything's okay. I'm worried about her feelings for Kasarian. From what you said, they sound close." Albert graced me with his first smile in days. "We both know how easy it is to develop feelings for your mark."

"I'm sure everything's fine," I said, not wanting him to worry. I'd hated having to tell him about Alexandra's less than enthusiastic response to our plan. "I told her to be cautious and not take any chances. That's why we haven't heard yet."

THE BICKERING CONTINUED the rest of the morning with Albert joining the fun. It was over stupid stuff like Varos getting jam in the peanut butter container, Albert not rinsing his dishes, and Brad eating the last donut, but the offended party always blew the transgression way out of proportion. Finally, I couldn't take it anymore. "I'm going for a walk," I called, depositing my lunch plate in the tiny kitchenette sink. Waiting around for Alexandra to hook us into the computer network was putting everyone on edge, including me. Despite its expanse, the warehouse practically hummed with our combined nervous energies. I needed air, or I was going to drown in it.

"You got your gun?" asked Albert. He sat hunched over the hotel schematics for the energy conference, reviewing his extraction plan for Alexandra.

"Yep," I said, shrugging on my jacket and opening the door.

A gust of cold air blasted me and despite the bite, I drank it in. A walk with some air that was fresh not stale was just what I needed. That and solitude.

"Hey, Little O, wait for me," said Varos, jogging over and grabbing his jacket. "You don't mind do you?"

*YES!* "Of course not."

Peering over his laptop, Brad eyed us suspiciously but said nothing. After all, what could he say? A 'don't go, I want you to be within listening distance at all times' wouldn't exactly fly. We were at the point where we had to trust each other, at least a little bit, whether we liked it or not.

I felt a tug of guilt as I left with Varos. Brad was right not to trust us. While our agenda paralleled Brad's, it wasn't the same. If we had our way, the CIA would be coming up a bit short on all available intel. While I thought it highly likely Albert would understand and forgive me for my duplicity, I wasn't so sure about Brad, and the thought worried me more than I liked. I was only just getting to know Brad, but he seemed to get me in a way the others didn't. I knew a lot of his insights were probably from his surveillance of me, which should have creeped me out, but strangely didn't. He felt like a friend I'd had for a long time but never met. A guardian angel, of sorts, only one with tactical training and an arsenal of weapons.

Varos turned to me when we were a few blocks from the safe house. "How do you feel about everything?"

I shrugged. "I'm wishing Alexandra would hurry up and get us the intel we need, but other than that, I'm okay. How about you? Feel like part of the Scooby gang yet?"

Varos snorted. "Yeah, right. They welcomed me with open arms."

I raised an eyebrow. "You expected otherwise?"

"No," said Varos, sighing. "Things are exactly how they should be. I'd trust Albert and Brad even less if they were nice."

I laughed quietly, as I ducked my head to a gust of wind whipping down the street. Such was the life of a spy, where mannered tolerance was trusted more than friendliness.

Varos and I fell into a comfortable silence as we walked. The farther we traveled from the safe house, the more crowded the sidewalk became until we entered a commercial shopping district with restaurants and stores. Given the repeated invasions, Olissa had little in the way of old heritage buildings, and the shopping district with its shiny glass and sleek, modern edges, mirrored how much of Olissa now looked. There were streaming fountains for making wishes and topiaries flanking every storefront. Only in the tiny towns dotting the countryside would you find any trace of the old and the ancient. Walking amongst the shops, it seemed strange an old country should have such a youthful face. It rang false somehow, but I guessed it was better than having no face at all.

The next storefront came into view, its window jam-packed with magnets, postcards, and other Olissan trinkets. Varos and I both stopped in our tracks. We eyeballed each other for a half second then veered into the store. A tourist shop? In Olissa? Olissa had rarely been stable enough for outside visitors. Although Brad and I had entered Olissa as "tourists" and I knew tourism to Olissa was becoming a thing, I hadn't expected an actual tourist shop with actual shoppers milling around inside.

We'd passed a few street posters touting Olissa as the hidden gem of Eurasia, but I'd thought that was wishful thinking on Olissa's part. But maybe not? "Look at this," I said, pulling out a T-shirt and holding it to my shoulders. It said Keep Calm and Stay Olissan Strong.

Varos walked over smiling. "Damn straight." He adjusted the shirt, so it no longer hung askew then bopped me on the nose. "Get it. You deserve a souvenir. If we pull this off, we won't be welcome back."

I picked up a stuffed three-headed dragon and waggled it at Varos. "For you. To keep you warm at night." My voice cracked as I tried to stuff down the emotion that came with potential exile.

"Well, maybe. Since I'm not getting any love from you," said Varos with a wink.

My heart skipped a beat, and I turned away to hide my blush. I found Varos' flirtation decidedly uncomfortable, and I didn't know whether it was because I was interested or because I wasn't. I was a one-guy kind of girl. Although I multitasked many things in my life, boys were not one of them. Grant and I weren't technically dating, but my focus was on him, at least for now. I didn't have room for anyone else. My head was constantly swimming with scenarios: mission scenarios, relationship scenarios, what-the-hell-I-was-going-to-do-when-Alexandra-comes-home scenarios, and frankly, it was all becoming a bit paralyzing.

Nudging me, Varos lifted a snow globe off a display shelf and flipped it over, so the *snow* pooled at the top of the glass dome. "I need one of these. So I can remember home when I'm on my island with my island girl." We both watched as he righted the snow globe and little flecks of white drifted down onto the Pretor River Bridge.

All of a sudden Varos whooped and set the snow globe back on its shelf. A millisecond later a small white box sailed in my direction. I narrowly caught it before it smacked into my chin. "Fudge," said Varos, hopping from foot to foot. "Olissan freaking fudge." Varos grabbed back the box I'd just caught and started shoving every other box on the shelf into a makeshift basket he'd made by folding up the hem of his shirt. He headed to check out whistling happily. I followed with my souvenir t-shirt.

Outside, we found a bench and Varos pulled out one of the fudge boxes. He opened it under his nose and moaned. "Oh my God, I've missed this stuff." He slid the box under my nose, and I sucked in a breath, nearly melting at the aroma of cardamom, mint, and chocolate. It was pure, heavenly delight. It was Olissa. It was home.

Varos and I both took a square and popped it into our mouths. We moaned in unison, and I laid my head on his shoulder.

"Orgasmic," he said.

I reached for another piece. "I'll take your word for it."

"Really?" said Varos, straightening. "You and Grant never did it? Or is he lacking in skills?"

"You know we didn't. You said it wasn't a good idea." I popped another piece of fudge in my mouth. If sex was as good as fudge, maybe I'd made a mistake by waiting.

Varos laughed. "I didn't think you'd listen to me. I knew you loved him; I thought for sure he'd get the better of you."

I pulled myself upright, feeling a surge of anger. "It was because I loved him nothing happened. I worried about what would happen if I let myself get that close."

Varos threw up his hands in surrender. "Sorry. Whatever the reason, I'm glad. You should get to be you the first time." Varos found my eyes. "Not Alexandra."

"I just hope to have sex before I die," I said, the words escaping before I realized quite what I was walking into. *Shit.* I grabbed another square of fudge and stuffed it into my mouth.

Varos chuckled. "I'm happy to take one for the team and help you with that. Although you'd better act fast, if you want to get me while I'm toned. This fudge is likely to make me fat again." Varos patted his stomach. "What do you think? Would you still love me if I porked back up?"

Not knowing if he was serious, I met his gaze. I hoped to find a mischievous, playful twinkle but was met with a hard edge. I'd walked right into this conversation with my sex comment. *Great. Just Great.* I wondered if somewhere deep down, I did want to test the waters with Varos? Because what girl doesn't need a stupid love triangle?

"It didn't stop me back at Perun," I said, deciding to just go with it. I tapped his forehead with a finger. "I'm more of a what's on the inside kind of girl."

Varos took my hand. "So I've got a chance?"

A heated blush took my cheeks. "If you want it." Embarrassed, I covered my cheeks and shook my head. I felt like a little schoolgirl.

"After we get Kasarian, I'm island bound. I've already got something set up off the grid. It's gorgeous, Little O. Really gorgeous. You'd love it." Varos touched the hand on my cheek and leaned in slowly for a kiss. Very slowly. He allowed me all the time in the world to pull back if I wanted. Except I didn't know what I wanted. I licked my lips in anticipation while my stomach clenched with guilt about Grant. I saw a hundred lives in those long seconds—lives lived with Varos and without. In some of them, we had a beautiful partnership—love, friendship, and understanding. In others, we unraveled and doomed each other to misery. The crazy I'd seen back in the States scared me. Although I didn't see it now, I knew it must be there somewhere, lurking. Waiting to be triggered. The longing in my heart, for something to grab onto and keep, ebbed and flowed with the chaos of possibilities. It sucked me in and spat me back out, over and over again. I was on a carnival ride that was, in turns, exhilarating and miserable as I was tugged one way then forced another.

I was pulling away, when Varos' hand snaked through my hair, and he found my lips. At his touch, my resistance slipped away. I was lost. All I felt was need. A need for something more than what I had. Something in front of me and tangible. Our first kiss had been so brief it almost didn't exist. This time, I gave in to the exquisite feel of his lips, soft but firm. In all the years as my handler, I'd never asked Varos about his life. It wouldn't have been appropriate, but judging from his kissing skills, there'd been at least a few women in his life. Part of me was jealous at the realization. He'd known almost everything about me. About Grant.

Driven by a need to finally know Varos, I kissed him harder. I wanted to steal back the years he'd kept from me. Varos tasted like fudge. Decadent. Kissing him was like being home. I savored him. I savored the knowledge that right now I was only me. I didn't know who the real me was, but I was here. Right now. Kissing a boy who I'd loved long ago and might … just maybe … be able to love again.

"I've missed you so much," whispered Varos, pulling away to kiss my neck, my jaw, my ear. His hot breath sparked a shiver down my spine. I closed my eyes and bathed in the feel of it. Varos knew me in a way Grant never could.

I felt drugged. Being with someone who knew the real me was a high, but we were sitting on a public bench … we were in the middle of an important mission. I teetered on the edge of an abyss, part of me wanting to fall, to escape into Varos. Going … Going …

"Oh my God," said someone behind me. "He's dead."

# NINETEEN

*DEAD? WHO'S DEAD?* I yanked myself back and lurched off the bench. "Sorry," I mumbled, turning toward the commotion.

A small group was gathering around a storefront, staring at a TV. "Aroyan's dead," said someone.

"A hit and run," said someone else.

Varos and I pushed our way into the growing crowd until we could see the image of a charred black car still billowing smoke and surrounded by police and an ambulance. The news ticker at the bottom of the screen raced by: *Presidential candidate and prominent businessman, Tarkan Aroyan, has been killed. Bystanders say it was a hit and run. Within the province of Yankin, a BOLO has been issued for a black Škoda van with a damaged right side. Please contact police immediately if spotted.* The ticker began again on repeat.

Varos and I looked at each other, then ducked our way out of the crowd.

"Well, there's no way that's a coincidence. You were right, Tarkan's Perun. One down and one to go," said Varos.

"Do you suppose it was the CIA or Vladik?" I asked,

thinking about my father. When Perun fissured, he'd landed on the side of Aroyan, and now the pony he'd picked to win the race was dead, potentially because of the intel I'd given Brad. If it was the CIA, I wondered if my dad would realize the mistake he'd made in telling me about Vladik? I might have just won my first game of chess against my dad. Too bad it was a game being played with people's lives; otherwise, I might have felt proud.

"Who knows? It doesn't matter does it?" He nudged me with his elbow and shot me a sly grin. "So where were we?"

I shook my head and stepped away. "I can't. Not right now." As much as I wanted to, I couldn't afford to lose myself. The image of Tarkan's smoldering car had driven home the stakes of this game. Trading a few emails with Grant was one thing, but starting something with Varos was entirely different. We were living together. Too much was on the line. My life wasn't a Hollywood movie. The only thing romance would get me was killed.

"Little O, wait a second."

I shot him a pleading look as he fell into step beside me. I felt like I'd just run an emotional marathon.

"I get it. Now's not a good time. I was there for the lessons at Perun, too. 'If you want to stay alive, then no real relationships and no real feelings.' But we'll both be walking away from this life, soon enough." Varos threw an arm around my shoulder and pulled me close, kissing the side of my head. "At least we know we've got chemistry. I'm a patient man. I can wait." My thoughts muddled, I stayed silent. "You felt it, didn't you? You felt the chemistry? It wasn't just me?"

I laughed, his worry bringing me out of my fugue. I leaned my head onto his shoulder. "It wasn't just you."

"Phew. You had me worried there." He squeezed my arm. "It's all going to be fine, Little O. You'll see."

I nestled into Varos' warmth. "Don't you think I've outgrown little? I'm as tall as you are."

"O then, for Odette, the beautiful white swan that steals men's hearts."

I snorted. "No offense, but you're not very good at playing the poet."

Although I couldn't see his face, I somehow knew Varos was rolling his eyes. He vibrated with a low down chuckle. "You wound me."

I needled him with my elbow. "Unlikely."

# TWENTY

POP. POP. POP. Shatter. *Hissssss.* My eyes sprang open as I bolted upright in bed. *What the hell? Was that a dream?* I looked side-to-side as I reached for the gun under my pillow. Brad was already out of bed, his gun drawn.

*Crap, not a dream.*

Brad flipped his cot over for cover, and I did the same, not that a thin mattress would do us much good. I pulled my gun up and looked for a target as I searched for Albert. The shattering sound had been our overhead lighting being taken out. The warehouse had skylights, though, and despite their grime, a smidgen of moonlight seeped in. There were six, and none were directly overhead, so I fired at each in quick succession, letting in more light. My ammo clip now empty, I ripped at the duct tape holding three clips under my bed and slid one into my gun and the other two into my underwear.

The hiss I'd heard was a smoke bomb set off near the door to cover our attacker's entry. It was dissipating quickly. Thanks to the additional light, I found Albert hunkered by the kitchenette behind the pantry door. He was firing an occasional shot and looked to be safe for the moment.

"I count six," yelled Brad.

"Confirmed," I said, aiming. I fired and landed a hit to the abdomen of one attacker, but the person only staggered back, then dove behind the sofa.

"Full flak," yelled Brad. "Head shots only."

*Head shots only? Oh God.* I hunched down closer to the floor. These weren't paper targets I was firing at but people. Sons and daughters. Maybe even mothers and fathers. My gut roiled as my old instructor's words came screaming back. "One man's terrorist is another man's freedom fighter." *Shit.*

Two smoke bomb canisters rolled our direction and exploded.

I pulled my pajama top over my nose and flattened myself to the floor. Although not as bad as tear gas, smoke bombs weren't fun and could easily send someone into a badly timed coughing fit. Trying to stay out of the eye-line of our intruders, Brad and I commando crawled out from behind our beds and away from the smoke only to ground to a halt seconds later when two pairs of shiny black boots appeared through the haze. A bullet hit in between Brad and me. A warning shot or a missed opportunity, I didn't know?

"Stop," said a gravelly voice, answering my question. "Stop where you are. Put your guns down and your hands up."

Still on our bellies, Brad and I lifted our hands from our guns in synchrony, leaving the weapons within easy reach should an opportunity arise.

The smoke dissipated further, and I saw Albert trading occasional shots with one of our attackers as the man slowly advanced on him, moving between points of cover. The warehouse didn't have much furniture, but it did have some large structural support beams that unfortunately offered great cover. Fighting for his life, Albert wouldn't be helping

Brad and me.

I was turning my attention toward Varos' side of the warehouse when I saw him launch a grenade at our makeshift lounge and the two combatants using the couch as cover. Kaboom.

Two down. Four to go. My fingers twitched over my gun, hoping the men with their guns trained on Brad and me would turn at the explosion. No dice. They'd been well trained. One turned to face the new danger while the other remained focused on us.

"Yoohoo," sang a voice. "Over here!" Varos spun out from behind his beam and opened fire on the two men guarding us. He hit the one facing him square in the chest, sending the guy flying backward. It wasn't a kill shot because the guy was in Kevlar, but it was enough to have Brad and me reaching for our guns, our fallen attacker providing both cover and an element of chaos. Brad fired and quickly dispatched the man still standing while I took aim at his fallen comrade. The hit dazed him for a moment, but then as if in slo-mo, he regained his wits. His muscles tensed. His finger found the trigger. He turned, finding my eyes. My heart thumped fast and loud in my ears. The electric impulses between my nerve synapses fired as if on overdrive. I tingled everywhere, from the tips of my ears to my toes. His gun raced to find me, to put me in its sights. Coming, coming, almost there, almost ...

I fired.

It's a rookie mistake to close your eyes when shooting a gun, but I wished I had. I would have given anything to unsee his body going instantly slack, his eyes open but dead. Where there was once life, now there was none. Because of me.

I didn't have time to ponder the horror before me,

though; that would come later. I scanned the room looking for another target, another person to kill. It was kill or be killed, and I didn't want to die. Brad was advancing on the man who had Albert pinned in the kitchenette while Varos traded gunfire with another hostile. We still had two hostiles and … shit … two more entering through the front door. Their team must have signaled for backup.

Varos' back was to our new guests putting him in danger. Using a support beam for cover, I fired on the hostiles. Bam. Bam. Dead. Bile rose in my throat. *Oh God. That was easy. Too easy. Who am I?*

It had been years since I properly trained in firearms combat, but everything I learned, it was all there, ready. I didn't need to think. All I needed, was to do. I felt like a robot. Everything around me was slow. So slow that I had more than enough time to react. To fire. To kill. *Oh God.*

I heard a cry of pain and spun as Varos fell. I raised my gun and fired. Again my eyes were open. Again I would have given anything not to see what I saw. A body dropping, now nothing more than an empty shell. This was sick. I was sick.

One hostile remained. Brad and Albert were both on him. I rushed to Varos and pulled him behind a beam then started to check for wounds. I'd only have a few seconds to staunch any vital bleeding before I needed to help Brad. Varos' arm was bleeding a torrent. I patted his chest down …

"What the ..."

Varos chuckled. "Kevlar baby, best pajamas ever," he said, sitting up with a twisted wince. "It's warm and toasty. Bullets still hurt like hell, though. I'm out of ammo. You got any .45 clips?" Varos looked at his bleeding arm, then shrugged. "God bless, adrenaline."

I sagged with relief as I ripped at the bottom of his shirt for a scrap to staunch the bleeding in his arm. "I've only got

9mm. Just stay here and sit tight." He yelped as I pulled the bandage taut.

"I'm not the only one bleeding," he said, nodding to my arm.

Sure enough, I was bleeding too. But I couldn't feel it. I studied my arm for a second not comprehending. How could I not feel it? Was adrenaline that powerful? Or was I a robot? A killing machine? It was during that one second I took to ponder my arm that I realized the gunfire had ceased. The warehouse was largely quiet except for the sound of thrown punches. Grunts. Curses. Fists hitting flesh.

Helping Varos hadn't taken long. Ten seconds? Twenty? But when I peered out from behind the beam, things had changed drastically. The gunman who had pinned Albert was down but now …

Brad was fighting with … my father? They'd stripped each other of their weapons. Two guns lay abandoned on the floor.

I raised my gun, searching for the perfect shot when I heard, "Wait!"

Keeping my gun on the brawl, I shifted my gaze and found Albert with his hands up, Mistress holding a Glock to his head. My blood turned to ice. Time stopped. The person I loved most in this world stood next to a contender for most reviled. I swung my gun toward Mistress.

"Tut. Tut. You might miss," she said. She tapped Albert's head with the barrel of the gun. "This brain would be a terrible thing to waste. Full of such good information. And besides …"

Mistress let her words trail away for dramatic effect, a smile seeping across her face. My trigger finger itched to end her, but I needed to steady myself first. Seeing Albert at her mercy jolted me. I could make the shot. I'd already made four shots just as hard only minutes before. I needed a second to center myself, though. "You wouldn't want to shoot your dear mother. Not after everything I've done for you."

I blinked. *What? Mother?*

My head spun, and I started to tremble. *She's toying with you,* I told myself. *She's trying to shake you, so you miss.* No matter what I told myself, I was a child again quaking under the heel of her boot. My gun hand wobbled. My vision clouded as my mind flashed to Perun and Mistress' hatred. To the nights she pulled me from bed in a drunken rage. I was always her target. No one else. Ever. The day he dropped me at Perun, my father said she'd love me, but why would she … unless. He'd thought a mother would have to love her daughter, but he was wrong. Very, very wrong. Yet she wanted me to be like her … clever as a fox.

To my left, someone howled, but I couldn't afford to look.

*Focus, Milena. Focus.*

I sucked in a breath, and my gun hand steadied. I sucked in another, and my brain cleared. I saw Albert. I saw the life I'd had with him. The love I'd had. I looked to Mistress and saw my life with her. There had been no love. Only fear. Loathing.

"Did you hear me, Milena? I'm your real—"

I fired, and Mistress dropped. She fell forward, knocking into Albert, sending him to his knees.

*But he's my Albert.* I raced to help him.

Behind me, Varos yelled something, but I couldn't make it out.

I was almost to Albert when he lurched to standing. His eyes were on Brad and my father, but then he was running toward me, his face contorted in terror. I skidded to a stop and turned toward the fight. Brad was on the ground, and my father had his hands back on the gun he'd lost.

He tracked me.

Aimed at me.

His face was raw, unadulterated pain and rage. All because I killed Mistress … his love?

And I had just stopped, making myself an easy target. *Shit.*

I raised my gun but knew I'd already lost. I'd never be fast enough.

Albert barreled into me as my father fired. Bang. Bang. Bang.

The first shot was true, the second and third wild, as Brad kicked my dad's legs out from under him.

Albert and I landed on Varos, who must also have been running for me. I found myself tangled in arms and legs. I couldn't find my feet. My body didn't seem to work, probably because my mind was akimbo. It tilted and whirled, swimming with thoughts of my father and mother. Thoughts that tried to drown me. Finally, I found the bottom and pushed to the surface coming up for a gasping breath. I raised my gun, searching for my father.

He was gone. The warehouse door flapped in the breeze, and Brad lay still at its base.

"Brad," I screamed. I was on my feet a second later and sliding into him a second after that. I searched for a pulse, surveying him for wounds. His cheek was swelling. One arm bled. His shirt was wet crimson, and I yanked it up with my free hand. I was still searching for a pulse. Finally, my fingers stumbled on a defined, steady beat. *Thank God.*

I was evaluating his chest wound when he grabbed my hand. "I'm fine."

"No, you're not. You've got a bullet in your abdomen. You're bleeding."

"A graze," said Brad, sucking in a shallow breath and

pulling himself up onto one elbow.

I snaked my hand around to his back, feeling for an exit wound. There wasn't one. *Not good.*

I pushed him back down. "It's not a graze. The bullet's still inside."

"O. You need to come here."

"Varos, I'll be with you in a second, I just—"

"O, come now," yelled Varos. "It's Albert."

I jerked my head and stumbled to my feet. Varos bent over Albert, his hands a shiny red. *NO! No. No. No.*

I scrambled across the room and took over applying pressure to the wound. Albert was conscious but pale. Really pale. "Stay with me, Albert. Stay with me." I looked at Varos, and he stared back, his face uncharacteristically somber. As rogue covert agents in a country we weren't welcome in, a hospital was out of the question. Varos knew that. I knew that. "Brad," I yelled. "Albert needs help. What do we do? What do we do?" I pressed harder on Albert's wound, but the blood still came. "Albert don't you dare die on me. You hear me, old man? Don't you dare die."

# TWENTY-ONE

"I KNOW A clinic," said Brad, stumbling to the door, hunched over and clearly in pain. "Get him in the car."

I choked down a relieved sob and moved to Albert's legs. Varos scooped Albert up under his arms as carefully as possible, and we shuffled to the door. With both of us injured, our movements were slow and jerky. "Faster," I wheezed, sidestepping Mistress' dead body. Without pressure to his wound, Albert was losing blood way too fast.

At the car, Brad had one door open, and I set Albert's legs down and dashed to open the opposite side. I crawled through and grabbed Albert's legs, sliding him inside. "Albert? Can you hear me?" His eyes flickered but didn't open. "You're going to be just fine. We're taking you to the doctor now."

"Hurry," I yelled, my tears starting to overtake me now. "Hurry. Hurry." Varos ran to the driver's side while Brad fell into the passenger seat and yanked open the glove box, digging out a burner phone.

"Where to?" asked Varos.

"Turn left. Then four blocks to the highway. It's the first

exit off the highway." Brad winced and stifled a groan as he dialed the phone. "You'll see the sign once you exit.

Someone must have answered because Brad said five words before hanging up. "It's Brad. I've got incoming." After that, he leaned back and closed his eyes.

Varos promptly whacked his leg. "Don't go to sleep. We need you."

Leaving Varos to keep an eye on Brad, I focused on Albert through eyes cloudy with tears. Good God, how had this happened? How had they found us? My whole body shook as shock set in. I was freezing cold, yet sweat poured off me. The pain in my arm was finally grabbing hold and twisting its knife, making me nauseous. My vision started to go dark, but I fought through it, letting myself sink into the pain like I did under the tattoo artist's needle. I let it wash over me and embraced it. Pain meant I was alive and sometimes being alive was victory enough.

We arrived at the clinic after an eternity. The veterinary clinic.

I stared at Brad. "You're kidding, right? We're not trusting Albert's life to an animal doctor?"

"There's no one here." said Varos, screeching into the parking lot. It was well past midnight.

"Sam's coming," said Brad. "There's a key in a fake rock by the potted plant outside the door." He glanced back at me. "Desperate times call for desperate measures. I've used Sam before. Don't worry."

Varos jumped out and went looking for the key. Brad started to pull himself around so he could see Albert, but I threw out a hand to stop him. "Don't move. You'll only make things worse."

Brad nodded with a sigh and stayed only partially turned. He leaned his head into the seat. "Please don't die, old man.

Please don't die," he muttered, closing his eyes. When they stayed closed for longer than a five count, I kicked his seat.

"Don't you dare fall asleep."

Brad grimaced, his lips twitching. "Jeez, you and Varos are tough. All I've got is a flesh wound. It hurts like hell, but I'll be fine. I just need to rest."

I wiped at my eyes. "And when did you pick up your medical degree? You have no exit wound. You have a bullet in your stomach." I looked down at my hands, now covered in blood. It was an angry crimson just like my mom's … like Sibel's had been. I was only a child, but the soldiers shot her right in front of me. Ever since I'd always hated the color red.

"Trust me, I've been wounded enough times to know when it's serious. This isn't. How's Albert doing?"

Albert was pale, a sheen of sweat coating his skin. His breaths were shallow. "He's going to be okay. He's a fighter," I said, in case he could hear me. *If I say the words, that makes them true, right?*

Varos opened the side door and reached in for Albert as another car peeled into the lot. "I've got it unlocked."

A pretty blonde launched from her car, dressed in a gown and heels. Sam? She joined Varos, taking Albert's left side. I followed behind, guiding his legs. "What happened?" she asked, glancing at Brad as he hobbled from the car. "Brad, are you okay?"

"Brad's fine. A flesh wound. Albert needs your help right now."

"Shit. This is the old man?" she asked, backing through the clinic door. Our entrance immediately woke the resident animals, triggering a cacophony of sound. Sam steered us through two sets of double doors and into the back room where we laid Albert onto a steel table. It was a table meant for animals and Albert's legs hung off the end. I resumed applying pressure to the wound and Sam began pulling out supplies. "Gunshot?" she asked.

"Yes." My voice was a croaking whisper. "He pushed me out of the way."

Sam kicked off her heels and pulled on a lab coat and a pair of latex gloves. "We'll need to roll him to check for an exit wound. Things will be a lot more interesting if there isn't one."

Varos and I rolled Albert so that Sam could get a clean view. "Damn," she said, nodding for us to roll him back. "I'm going to need blood. Do you know his blood type Brad or is anyone O neg?"

Already in knots my stomach managed to ball up even more, which hardly seemed possible. "I'm O neg," I said. "Take as much as you need. Take all of it. Varos you apply pressure to the wound."

Sam looked from me to Brad; her eyebrows arched in question. "An exact match would be best. There are antibodies in O neg that could react with Albert's blood."

Brad shook his head. "He's A negative. I'm A positive." He looked to Varos.

"I'm AB negative," replied Varos, putting a calming hand on my shoulder before shifting into position over Albert.

I began searching for the needles and tubing we needed, making a mess of Sam's shelves. By now my eyes were burning so bad from all the crying; everything I tried to read was a blur. "My blood is our only shot. Come on. We need to hurry, damn it."

I flinched when two hands found my shoulders. "You need to stay calm," said Brad, his voice soft. "Freaking out isn't going to help Albert." Brad reached for a paper box and flipped the cover, revealing a box of needles. He flipped another cover to reveal some tubing. He'd definitely been here, and I wondered what had brought him to the clinic the last time.

"Brad, you good to hook her up?" asked Sam.

"M's been shot. I'm not sure—"

I snatched the needles and tubing from him. "I'm fine. Let's do this."

Brad grabbed my arm. I jerked away, but he grabbed it again, this time holding tight. If his grip was anything to go by, he had time before he needed Sam's attention. I found and held his gaze, pleading for his understanding. "I need to do this. He got shot saving me. He's my family, please …"

Brad opened his mouth then clamped it shut, dropping my arm. In that moment his eyes said volumes, but not in a language I could interpret. The muscles in his jaw twitched tightly as he stared into the deepest parts of me.

*Looking …*

*Finding …*

"I'll hook her up."

# TWENTY-TWO

DESPITE MY BEST intentions, sleep took me sometime during the blood transfer. I was awake and listening to Sam's commentary as she worked, and then I was out.

I woke with a jolt. As one might expect, my dreams hadn't been good, my father featuring heavily. Next time I saw him, he was dead. I'd sent Mistress to hell, and I'd send him too. They could both dance with the devil for all eternity.

As the fog of my dream cleared, I heard an "Ouch. God damn it. You're not even trying to be nice," then an "I offered you drugs, but you said no. Quit whining and stay still."

Laid out on a surgical table, I levered myself upright. In the process, I noticed my arm was wrapped tight with white gauze and medical tape. They must have given me drugs because I wasn't feeling much in the way of pain.

"Don't get up too quickly," said a voice. My eyes wandered the room looking for the owner. I found Sam standing over Brad, who was laid out on a bench top. She was stitching him up. "You gave quite a bit of blood. You'll be dizzy."

"How's Albert?" I asked, sliding slowly off the table. As soon as my feet hit the ground, my head spun and my knees buckled. I had to clutch the table for support.

From somewhere behind me, Varos appeared and offered his hand. I took it, and he led me over to a chair. He had a matching bandage on his arm.

"Albert made it through surgery," said Sam. "I managed to get the bullet out, but it shredded his spleen. I had to remove it."

"You can live without a spleen, though, right?" I asked, my mind racing over my limited knowledge of human organs. People got their spleens removed sometimes, didn't they? It was like an appendix?

"You can live without it, but the spleen helps with bacteria removal. If he survives, he'll be more susceptible to infection."

My heart clenched. *If he survives? He had to.* "What are his chances?" I asked, my voice a hoarse whisper, my eyes already fighting to hold back tears. *Damn it. Keep it together. Keep it together.*

"There," said Sam, patting Brad on the shoulder and leaning in to kiss his forehead. "You're done. Be careful and don't pull out my stitches, okay?" Sam turned. "Milena, honey, I'm a vet. I don't honestly know. If he wakes up in the next twenty-four hours, he has a chance."

I glanced at Albert. They'd pushed two examination tables together, and he was laid out flat. I watched the rise and fall of his chest. He looked so old. So small. The sight was a cannonball to the chest, and I had to fight to breathe.

"He's a tough old man," said Brad, finding his feet and shrugging on his bloodied shirt. "He'll be fine. I'm sure of it. We have bigger concerns, like how the hell your dad and Mistress found us. Until we know that, none of us are safe." Brad's gaze shifted to Varos.

"Did you forget the part where they shot me?" said Varos. "I'm not your leak."

When Brad seemed less than swayed by Varos' argument, I chimed in. "He warned me about my Dad taking aim. He and Albert both tried to save me. It's not him."

"Who is it? Because I know it's not you, me or Albert. Varos, maybe they picked you up coming into the country and followed you to the safe house. How careful were you?"

"Careful. I entered Olissa disguised as an old man, on a fresh passport. It wasn't me."

"Well, they tracked us down somehow." Brad's expression was sour. By contrast, Sam's face brightened momentarily before falling flat again. She opened her mouth then shook her head, closing it again. She turned away, busying herself with loading the autoclave.

"Sam, what were you going to say," I asked, too curious to let it go. "If she had an idea about how they tracked us, I wanted to hear it."

"I read a lot of spy books," said Sam, glancing at Brad and blushing. "But I'm sure it's nothing."

"What's nothing?" Brad and I said in unison.

Sam waved us off, flustered. "You're going to think I'm an idiot."

Brad softly touched her arm, his fingers lingering. "No, we won't. I promise."

Sam sighed, her eyes going skyward as if she was saying a quick prayer. "After I stitched up Milena's arm, I did an exam to check for other injuries, and I found a rash on her neck. I sometimes see the same reaction on animals when—"

"Flea bites," I said, rubbing my fingers over the scabby bumps.

Varos grabbed my wrist, stopping me. With his free hand, he brushed my hair off the bites.

I squirmed. "What are you doing?"

Varos yanked my arm to hold me still. "How long have

you had these?"

"Since Ork was shot," I replied, yanking away. I stepped out of my seat and nearly collapsed. Sam was right. I was seriously dizzy after the blood transfer. Big movements were out of the question. I stumbled to the exam table and propped myself up trying to look nonchalant, but my stomach dipped as concern gripped me. Something in my brain went click.

Click. Click. Click.

I had almost regained my equilibrium when Brad was at my side, pushing my head forward and my hair up. "You noticed the *bites* after the run in with your dad, not before?"

"Yeah. Sooooo …"

Click. Click. KABOOM!

My father had me by the neck at two points during our fight. One little jab with a ring or something similar and he could have injected me. There was too much going on. I was already in pain from the blows to my head. I wouldn't have noticed a small prick.

"NO! No, no, no!" I covered my neck and stepped away, only to have my knees give way as my head spun. Brad grabbed me before I hit the floor and steered me back to the seat I'd vacated. "He tagged me with a radio tracker didn't he? The plan was always for me to escape. It was me. I'm the reason they found us. I'm the reason Albert might die." I gazed up at Brad, barely able to see him through my tears. I grabbed his shoulders. "He didn't slip when he mentioned Vladik, did he? He wanted me to kill him; that's why he let me go." I dug my fingers into Brad's shoulders. "Did the CIA kill Aroyan in a hit and run? Did I get my dad's boss killed? Is that why he came after us before we got Vladik?" I grabbed my mouth, my stomach soured by the poison of truth. "I'm going to be sick."

Before I knew it, Brad had a bucket in my lap. I spent the

next several minutes dry heaving while Varos patted my back and Brad tried to talk me off the ledge.

"You couldn't have known," he murmured. "I saw your neck. I thought they were flea bites too. I've never seen that kind of reaction to a tracker insertion." Brad's hand found my knee and his thumb started to rub back and forth and then in a circle. Strangely, it wasn't Brad's words that brought me back; it was that thumb.

Back and forth.

Around and around.

His touch was relaxing. Focusing on it, I was finally able to stuff back my nausea. Wet with sweat, Brad brushed back the hair plastered to my face. Somehow he managed a smile. "Look on the bright side. We're all still here, and you managed to take out Mistress."

In spite of it all, I laughed. It was only for a second, but I laughed. It fell away almost as soon as it appeared, like a shooting star. It was a split second of humor invading an abyss of painful chaos.

"I killed my mother."

Brad's eyes widened as if confused, but then understanding flashed and he gave a pitying nod.

"You and Albert knew about Mistress, didn't you? You knew what she was to me?"

Brad shook his head. "About Mistress? No. We only knew you weren't Sibel Rokva's daughter. We compared your DNA to Amalya's, and it showed no biological relationship. We figured your mother must be someone within Perun, but we had no idea who."

I'd stopped crying, but my tears returned with a vengeance as I remembered my encounter with Amalya. *I cannot forgive you ... Not after what your mother did. After what she took from me.* I'd been so confused, wondering what my mother could have done. I now realized she was speaking not of her daughter but Mistress. "Bucket," I whispered.

A clean bucket materialized just as I started dry heaving again. My stomach twisted bringing up bile, flecked with red. Blood.

"You need to calm down and get hold of yourself," said Varos. Going for tough love, he slapped me on the back and said, "Man up."

Wiping a sleeve across my sweat drenched head, I looked up and caught Brad giving Varos a death stare. Knowing I'd caught him, Brad put a hand on each shoulder and eyed me until I finally looked back. "Breathe," he said. Brad sucked in a breath and let it out slowly, nodding for me to follow. I tried to mimic him, but my first attempt caught in my throat and I gagged. "Breathe," said Brad. "Slow and easy."

I wiped at my face as I tried for another slow breath. Brad pulled his sleeve down and joined me in clearing the tears. I managed to suck in a full breath and tried for another. I was slowly exhaling when Amalya's words snuck back in. *Not after what your mother did. After what she took from me.*

I don't know whether Brad saw the panic in my eyes or the return of my white knuckle bucket clutching, but he grabbed my chin. "Breathe," he said firmly. "Look at me and breathe. You are okay."

"I th-think m-m-mistress k-killed m-m-myyy m-m-mo … S-sibel," I managed to stutter. I felt so cold. My teeth chattered. I couldn't stop shivering. I was drowning in knowledge, and there was nowhere to swim. No escaping it.

Brad said something, but I couldn't make it out. He sounded so far away. Like he was in another room with the door closed. "W-w-what?"

I focused on Brad's mouth, trying to read his lips. I think I grabbed his face, to steady him so that I could make out his words. His lips went in and out of focus. He waved an arm wildly, and I followed it to Sam. She approached, brows furrowed. Her mouth moved, but like Brad, I couldn't hear her. I narrowed my eyes trying to get a clear view of her lips. *What did they say?* A big needle and syringe appeared out of thin air, and I flailed back in my seat, kicking out with my legs.

Brad toppling backward was the last thing I saw before I felt the pinch of the needle. From there, my limbs turned heavy as blackness crept in from whatever sedative Sam had used. I tried to fight my way through it but couldn't find a path. No matter how hard I struggled, I kept going …

down,

down,

down.

Deeper and deeper.

Until I reached …

the void of nothingness.

# TWENTY-THREE

I WOKE IN a soft downy bed. I felt both exhausted and like I'd slept a million hours. Birds chirped happily outside and without moving a muscle, I could see them flit past through lace curtains. Where the hell was I? This wasn't the warehouse or the vet clinic. It looked like an honest to goodness home. There was floral wallpaper, a big wooden dresser, and someone had tucked me under a pretty rose colored comforter. For a second my adrenal system kicked in at the strange locale but then sputtered out. Waking from sedation, I didn't have the energy to fight or flee. It was all I could do to keep blinking my eyes; the lids felt so heavy.

"Oh good, you're up! I was beginning to think they'd knocked you out with a horse tranquilizer," said a raspy voice. If I'd been feeling like my normal self, I would have leaped from the bed and landed in a fighting stance, but as it was, I merely rolled my head to the side and hoped the grim reaper wouldn't be staring back at me. Albert was propped up by pillows, reading the copy of Nicholas Nickleby I'd given him for Christmas. There was still an IV attached to his arm, and he looked considerably less than healthy, but he was alive and talking. Thank God.

I reached a lazy arm out for Albert's hand. "I love you so much. You don't know how scared I was. Thank you for saving me but don't do it again, okay?"

Albert smiled and squeezed my hand. "I'd laugh, but that'd hurt too much." We lay there for a minute, our mouths quirked in half smiles, reveling in the fact we were both alive. We lay there until Albert's face grew somber. "I'm sorry about what you had to do. That couldn't have been easy."

"My real mom died years ago."

I smiled at Albert as my mind wandered back to my childhood and the day the soldiers came. The day my mother died. Mistress hadn't been there, but the soldiers appeared out of nowhere. There had been some recent border skirmishes, and I'd assumed the soldiers were foreign, but now that I thought about it, I'd heard no news of any deaths in the weeks following her murder. I'd been too young to consider what that meant but now … I was at Perun two weeks later. Had my mother refused to give me up? Had she paid with her life? I vaguely remembered tension between her and Father in the weeks before she died. I'd always loved my mother, but I now realized what a true saint she'd been. I wasn't hers by blood, but she never once treated me as anything other than her daughter. There was no bitterness. Only love. I glanced at Albert taking in all his wonderful, grandfatherly glory. I was a lucky girl to have had two saints in my life. Sure my biological parents were evil, vile human beings, but at least I'd had Sibel and Albert. No telling how I would have turned out otherwise.

"Where is everyone?" I asked. "How long have I been out?"

"Twenty-four hours. How are you feeling?"

I glanced at my throbbing arm, and my neck twinged

sharply. "Ouch," I said, my fingers racing for the offending part of myself. I found a neat line of sutures.

"While you were out, Varos removed the tracker with Sam's help. You're clear."

I'd almost brought the whole mission down with my stupidity. I'd almost lost Albert because of some Goddamn radio tracker. "How are you feeling?" I asked, appraising him.

"Not bad at the moment. Sam has me on some great painkillers. It'll be awhile before I'm a hundred percent, though." Albert searched my face. "Which means I'm going to need a favor."

I nodded, understanding. "I'll get Alexandra out. You don't have to worry. Whatever you need, I'm your girl."

"Thank you," said Albert, leaning back into his pillow and closing his eyes. He readjusted his sitting position with a wince. "The boys were able to salvage a computer from the warehouse. Kasarian's data is rolling in."

"Alexandra did it?"

"She did it," said Albert, a lazy grin overtaking his face, his eyes still closed.

Although my heart skittered, I smiled, genuinely happy. After almost losing Albert, seeing him alive and happy filled me with contentment. I would get Alexandra out for him. She had done right by Albert, and I would do right by the both of them.

# TWENTY-FOUR

LEAVING ALBERT TO nap, I left our shared room in search of some food. I found a photo of Sam in the hallway, thus answering the question of where I was. The kitchen was empty, so I helped myself to a banana and a chunk of cheese from the fridge, hoping Sam wouldn't mind. I was eyeing a bag of nuts in the pantry when I heard muffled sounds down the hall. I followed them keen to show everyone I was awake and no longer melting down. I'd had a brief lapse in composure at Sam's office, and it would not be happening again. My suspicions about Mistress and my mother's death were shoved in a vault to be dealt with never. Both were dead, and if Mistress had killed my mother, I was glad my bullet was the one to end her, no matter what DNA we shared. The thought of ever being in that woman's womb sickened me.

I rounded a corner and walked past a study with the door open. I backpedaled seeing Varos standing with an empty glass pressed to the side wall, his ear to the base.

"Are you five-years-old?" I asked, not bothering to lower my voice.

"I was in a pinch. Don't mock," whispered Varos,

beckoning me closer. He withdrew his ear from the glass and motioned for me to take his position. "This concerns you. Brad's on the phone with the CIA."

I raised an eyebrow but took his spot, pressing my ear to the glass.

The muffled voice coming from the adjacent room sharpened instantly. Who needs high tech spy gear when low tech will do? In spite of myself, I smiled at Varos.

He didn't smile back, instead encouraging me to focus with an urgent nod to the wall.

I rolled my eyes but tuned into the voice.

"Yes." Pause. "Yes, I understand." Pause. "No, Sir. The data is coming in as we speak." Pause. "Where are we with the immunity deals, I spoke to you about?" Pause. "Uh huh. Yes, that's right."

My heart started to thud so loudly I had to really focus to hear. Had our immunity deal come through? I thought of Grant and wondered if he'd emailed again. Maybe I'd have some good news to tell him.

"Yes." Pause. "Yes, the plan is to extract Alexandra at the Istanbul Energy Conference. She's close to being done with her work on cold fusion." Pause. "Having her back in the States would be a boon for the country. She's very smart."

I glanced at Varos, who watched me intently. "Anything?" he mouthed.

I shook my head, the juices in my stomach stirring uncomfortably. I hated having my fate in someone else's hands. I wanted Albert able to go home after all this was over. And I wanted to go home too.

For Albert.

Grant.

Martine.

College.

It surprised me I now thought of the US as home. Olissa had always been home, but somewhere along the line that had changed without me realizing.

"Thank you, Sir. I'll tell Albert about the deal for him and Alexandra. He'll be so pleased. Now about—"

"Sir!" said Brad, loudly. "No, I don't understand. She'll never agree to inform on her friends. She's already brought in her old Handler to help keep that information from us."

I started to sweat, my heart racing. He knew.

"Yes, Sir. That makes sense, but I'm telling you that she won't give up the cadets in order to come home. She wants to be with Albert, but she won't make that trade."

"I understand that, but trying to strong-arm her for additional information isn't going to get you anywhere. This was Milena's plan to get Vladik. Her intel made it possible. I know you want the names of the other sleepers, but she deserves immunity just for Vladik and—"

A heavy pause.

"Sir, you're being unreasonable."

My heart stuttered, and my stomach somersaulted, bile rising into my throat. I pulled away from the wall and handed Varos the glass. "Thanks," I said, turning to the door.

Varos grabbed my arm and reached a hand out, probably seeing the crushing disappointment on my face—the look that said there would be no immunity deal. He tucked a stray piece of hair behind my ear. "Come with me," he said. "We can sip Mai Tais and get a tan for the rest of our lives. Forget about all this spy crap."

I studied him, his chocolate eyes, full of hope and longing, reeling me in. I didn't have to be alone. I had options.

I searched in his eyes for what a future with him might hold. I wondered if I could be happy sipping Mai Tais day-in and day-out. I liked a good vacation just as much as the next girl but …

Varos tucked a hand around my neck, drawing me near and making my nervous system spark. Little jolts of electricity snaked down my arms, legs and spine until I hummed. His lips brushed my lips, my cheek, my ear. "Be with me," he whispered, his hot breath skating over my ear, causing me to shiver.

"I … I … I …" Varos' lips grazed my neck, lighting it on fire. "Varos, I … my mom … Mistress … everything …"

I reached a hand out to Varos, whether to push him away or bring him near, I didn't know. Goosebumps pricked under my fingers as he shuddered, stepping back. He coughed once, clearing his throat. "Are you okay about what happened? I know you've never killed anybody."

"Okay that Mistress is dead? Yeah, I'm pretty cool with that."

"And about the others you killed?"

I grimaced, the food I'd eaten turning sour in my stomach. *Way to kill a moment, Varos.* "It was self-defense. What was I supposed to do? Cower in the corner while you guys got shot?"

"I know you O. You're not cold-blooded. It's okay to feel something—"

"No, it's not," I said, nearly yelling. "Not right now, it isn't. If I let myself feel something … anything … I'll shut myself in a closet and never come out. I never wanted …" I looked down at my clothes, my hands, my feet. "I never wanted to be this."

I tried to skirt my way around Varo, my hands beginning to shake. I didn't even know the faces of the men I'd killed or the names. It somehow seemed like I should know those things. I'd been so in the zone when I'd killed them; it was like I was some machine in a video game, a bio-enhanced robot girl. The thought sickened me. What had Perun turned me into with all their training? Shouldn't I have at least been rusty? Shouldn't it have been harder to pull the trigger?

Varos grabbed my arm, and I closed my eyes to try and regain my composure. I felt the heat of his breath as he drew closer. It smelled of cinnamon and … fudge. Olissan freaking fudge. A shiver betrayed me right before Varos kissed the corner of my mouth. Desperate for a distraction from my looming feelings of guilt and the disappointment of the failed immunity deal, I turned so our lips would meet.

Only they didn't.

Varos was there, tantalizingly close, but he only leaned his forehead into mine. "You need to make a decision. I don't want to be your distraction." His thumb stroked my cheek. "I want you to make a choice. A real choice that you've had time to think through. I know things are crazy right now, so I want you to take some time. Do what you need to do to decide. Make a list. Do whatever. But make this decision for you."

# TWENTY-FIVE

WANTING TO GET as far from the awkwardness with Varos as possible, I headed back to the kitchen and nearly crashed into Sam. She stopped me at arm's length and gave me the once over before smiling. "You're looking so much better. How are you feeling?"

Easily five inches taller than Sam, I peered down into her kind green eyes. I opened my mouth to answer, but the words didn't come.

Sam touched my arm gingerly. "What's wrong, sweetheart?"

I gathered myself and shook my head. There would be no deal. No immunity. Albert and Alexandra could go home but not me. "Nothing. I'm fine." I fought for a smile and when my mind wandered to a vision of Albert back at his farmhouse, the house that was home to generations of Gastones, that's when I finally found it. It came easy then. Albert was alive and would go home. He'd live out his life in the country he loved with the only true family he had left. I gathered Sam into a hug. "Thank you for saving him," I said, squeezing her tight. "He means everything to me. Everything."

Sam patted my back with a small laugh. "You're welcome. Are you okay? You're shaking."

I pulled back, wiping at my misty eyes. I straightened, squared my shoulders, and smiled again. "I'll be fine. I am fine." I found Sam's eyes for a second and nodded. "I'm going to get some fresh air." Skirting around her, I spotted a laptop on the kitchen table where there hadn't been one before. "Is that your computer? Could I borrow it?"

Installing myself on the porch swing, I opened the laptop. I couldn't think of anything with Varos until I did right by Grant. I pulled up my email, a part of me hoping Grant hadn't written back, that my admission about trying to kill my father had scared him away. But no such luck. His email was there waiting, offering certain torture. The arrow hovered over it, beckoning. I closed my eyes and clicked with a trembling hand.

Dear She Who Must Not Be Named,

You wrote back! Part of me didn't believe you would. Not after all my questions. Thank you for answering them, though. You did your worst and didn't scare me away! I'll be honest; your words did scare me, but not in the way you might think. I'm more scared for you than scared of you. I don't understand what kind of Father could give their child away to a network of spies to become a trained killer. If you see your father again, please be careful. Your life isn't worth his. Remember that.

LOL, I thought my questions were tough.

I wrote the poem after the homecoming dance and your

birthday dinner. I think it came from meeting Martine for the first time. She's so different from the friends we share, but you seemed more at home with her than anyone, including me. I couldn't figure out why you had kept a person, who was clearly so important to you, a secret. Part of me was mad, but mostly I was worried about you. Worried about why you felt you needed to lie and keep secrets. The poem sprung from that, from me trying to decipher the enigma that is you.

What scares me the most about you? I think it's the fear that no matter how much you want to, you'll never be able to make it to the other side. And by the other side, I mean normal life. You've been through so much; I worry you won't be able to shed the spy skin you wear. I worry you'll find regular life suffocating and boring. I worry you'll want James Bond, and all I'll be able to give you is Phil on *Modern Family*.

You want spy book recommendations, huh? I just finished *The Intelligencer* by Leslie Silbert. I think you'd like it. It's got a kick-ass female spy and weaves a modern-day spy story with a historical one. I'm now reading *Red Sparrow* by Jason Matthews, which is both awesome and scary as hell. The technology spies have these days is ludicrous. It makes it hard to sleep at night. Big Brother is alive and well. Eek.

Now that I've answered your questions, I have a few more for you. Drumroll …

1. After you retire from spying, what do you want to do when you grow up?

I read the question, then reread. What did I want to do? I sucked in a breath and wiped my snotty nose on my sleeve. I had no freaking idea. I'd been singularly focused for years, and now I had no focus beyond my present mission to bring Perun down.

2. How did you and Martine become friends? What do you like best about her?

I choked back a laugh. What didn't I like about her? She was free. Unbound. Unworried. She was everything I craved to be.

3. What were you like as a little girl?

Sweet. Innocent. Someone you could have loved.

4. When did you fall in love with me?

I guarded against loving you for so long; I don't honestly know. My love appeared one day, fully formed and a mystery even to me.

5. Be honest, would you be satisfied with a normal life?

Yes! It's all I've ever wanted.

6. Where is home for you? The States? Olissa?

I don't know anymore. The US, I think.

7. Do you have any more secrets I should know?

I don't know if I'm ever going to be able to get over you. Varos was my first love, but I fear you might be my true love.

Write soon!
Agent 00

After reading his email, I wished with every fiber of my being that Grant and I had a future. I ached with love for him. But I would never betray my fellow cadets so there would never be an immunity deal for me. As much as I wanted one, Grant and I didn't have a future. It was best to end things now. Hitting reply, I started to write.

Dear Grant,

I didn't get the immunity deal. I'm not coming back home. I love you, and I'm sorry for everything. It means the world to me you wanted to give us a shot, but there's no point. There will never be an us. Only me and you.

I want you to have the most amazing life for both our sakes. Don't ever give up on your photography. Your work is beautiful. Passionate. Stunning. Your work is you!

I won't be checking this email again, so go live your life and forget about me. I'll be doing the same.

Love,
M.

With a shaking finger, I clicked send before I could change

my mind. The end of my relationship speeding away, I closed my eyes and sucked in a breath to stifle my sob. It had been a long shot, but it had been a shot. I thought I'd guarded myself against high hopes, but as the weight of what I'd just done bore down on me, I knew I'd been deluding myself. I wanted the fairytale and got life instead. Fairytales didn't happen to people like me. I stared at my screen wanting to yank back my email. I wanted to stave off the end for another month, a week, a day, a minute.

I swiped at the tears pouring out of my eyes as if they were faucets. Goddamn, why had I read his email? It only made it worse. I signed-off and closed the computer. My chest was so tight; I curled in on myself and folded sideways onto the swing. It was the same as before. That morning Grant had screamed and thrown me out of the house. It was the same. I was empty inside, and all that filled the void was pain. It crept through my nerves and captured all of me. It stamped down everything I had that was good.

Albert was alive.

Albert could go home.

It crushed those happy bits of me until everything I saw, everywhere I looked there was a smoldering black cloud, ready to rain down bullets and pummel me.

# TWENTY-SIX

WRECKED BY SAYING goodbye to Grant, I needed to get away from Sam's house for a while and decided on a walk. We would head to Turkey tomorrow and by the next day, if all went according to plan, Alexandra would be extracted. I had two days' worth of plans and after that … nothing was on my horizon. I bowed my head to the wind and walked with no clear path or destination in mind.

Why had I let myself hope? It was stupid to think the CIA would offer me a deal. Busted sleeper agents didn't get offers to stay in the country they were sent to spy on, especially when they wouldn't name names. They got prison or in the best case, deportation. Although Albert had wronged the US by harboring me for so many years, he had a genius granddaughter going for him, and Alexandra wouldn't want to come to the US without him.

As I walked onward, the wind kicked up another notch, and I scrunched down into my coat surveying the streets before me. Everywhere I looked seemed foreign. Olissa was now a modern, architectural mecca, shiny and new and not at all like I remembered. The wind was the only thing that tugged at my memories. I'd come in from playing with my brothers, my cheeks so wind burned they'd be hot to the touch. Mom … Sibel … would line the three of us in a tidy row and slather on lanolin lotion, kissing our foreheads, noses, and mouths when she finished. She had been my mother when I had none. Sibel Rokva not Mistress. I shook my head. Good God, I didn't even know Mistress' real name. She was that much of a stranger to me. Mistress being my biological mother was a slap across the face. No. Something more, it was a blinding eye gouge. I closed my eyes to protect myself.

Bang.

Bullseye.

An image of Mistress slumping onto Albert replaced my mother's kisses and with it came a fire inside my belly, a flame made of old fears and hate. Lots of hate. Suddenly, I wasn't cold anymore.

Soon after leaving Sam's house, I noticed a tail. A moment of panic had ensued before I realized it was Brad. I quickened my pace and tried a few evasion techniques, but Brad stayed on me. Never too close but never completely gone. He seemed content to follow, so I quit making our lives hard and tried to ignore him and find my center.

Except I couldn't. Something inside me hummed. Simmered. Maybe it was my hate for Mistress. My father. Perun. My circumstances. The warm embrace of it turned to something smothering. I kept shaking my arms as I walked, trying to release the tension. To Brad, it probably looked like I was having spasms. At one point I stopped and shook out my whole body, my frustration growing. My simmer had notched up to a boil.

And then I saw the light.

It was green neon. A tattoo parlor.

I made a beeline for it, not even caring Brad would follow. That Brad might tell Albert.

The door chimed as I walked in and a heavy guy with a big white beard and ink sleeves smiled at me from behind the front desk. He looked like a tattooed Santa and had the jovial, twinkling eyes to boot.

"I'd like a tattoo," I said, stepping up to the desk.

"You've come to the right place," said Santa, pushing forward an ideas book.

I pulled up the side of my shirt and angled toward him. "I don't need the book. I just need you to add another bird to my flock."

"No problem," said Santa as the door chimed and Brad sauntered in. I tensed half expecting him to try and haul me out by my hair.

Instead, he sidled up next to me. "Hey, Aco. Does Lana have time for some fill work?"

Santa nodded. "She's free. You can head back."

I gaped at Brad, and he offered a wicked smile in return. "What?" he said. "You're not the only one who likes ink and work often takes me to Olissa."

I followed Brad into the back room where Lana greeted him with a smile. "Let me have a look," she said, at which point Brad shrugged off his jacket and shirt. My eyes nearly bugged out. On Brad's back was a huge Phoenix with wings spread, running from his waist to his shoulders. How had I not seen it before? It was incomplete but gorgeous with almost iridescent greens, blues, and reds. It was the kind of tattoo that took months of painstaking labor to complete. "We'll do the oranges today," said Lana, nodding to his stomach. "What happened there? You okay?"

"Had a rough couple days. Maybe we'll keep this a short session." Lana nodded and started her prep while Brad took a seat.

"You can sit here," said Santa patting a seat near Brad. "Or we have a private room if you'd rather?"

"Here's fine." I pulled off my coat, letting it drop onto the pile of clothes Brad started, then added my shirt. Standing there, bare except for my bra, I felt Brad's eyes on me, studying my tattoos. His look was unapologetic, and I found myself surprisingly unselfconscious.

His eyes eventually wandered to mine. "They're beautiful."

Holding his gaze, I ran a nervous hand over my flock. "Thank you. Yours too."

Brad nodded, the right side of his mouth crooking upward in a half-smile. "I won't tell Albert."

I laughed, "Thanks. I appreciate it." I headed for Santa, who was gloved up and ready, but Brad snagged my arm. He said nothing, his eyes following the birds as they soared along their path. A tentative finger came to my broken birdcage, and I shuddered as he traced its outline. His half-smile turned into a full frown as he released me.

I took my seat and lowered myself against the slanted chair rest. As Lana started on Brad's oranges, Santa drew several small black birds on a blank sheet of paper, and I picked which I wanted, a little swallow shooting forward like an arrow, shooting beyond the bad news I'd just received. Santa flicked the switch on his needle, and I sighed heavy at the impending release. Thanks to Brad, more than bottled up hate came out of me, and I smiled thinking of his hands on me, tracing my birdcage. It meant nothing, a mere moment of appreciation and sadness, but what a moment. For a brief second, something had clicked. Rotated. Burned. I finally believed Brad when he said he knew me.

I was done in ten minutes, my thirteenth little bird safely etched into my skin, forever and always. You'd think that after thirteen birds, my times with the needle would have blurred together, but each was sharp in my memory. I remembered what I did each day and what led me to the chair. This day would be no different. It was the day my dreams died. The day my little tattoo secret came to light. The day when I sat with a friend to face the needle. A friend who understood.

Feeling more in control, I decided to wait for Brad instead of taking the opportunity to ditch him. I took a seat opposite and smiled. "How much longer?"

"Another fifteen," said Lana.

"You going to play nice and wait for me?" asked Brad, surprised.

"Yeah, I don't have anything else to do but head back, and I'm in no rush."

Brad's eyebrows furrowed. "Head back? You're almost there."

"Almost where?"

"The Olissan Royal Ballet Theatre. When you turned left a mile back, I was sure that's where you were headed."

I shook my head. "Nope. Just wandering aimlessly."

Brad reached for my hand, but Lana tapped his arm warning him not to move. "Tut. Tut. You'll mess me up."

"Sorry Lan," said Brad, then to me, "It's Friday night, there's probably a ballet on. Why don't we grab tickets?"

"You want to take me to the ballet? I'm not exactly dressed for it."

"I don't look so great myself. I don't mind if you don't?"

I bit my lip. Did I want to torture myself with the ballet? With what could have been? Then again, my day was already shaping up to be pretty bad; maybe I should go with it and embrace the suck.

# TWENTY-SEVEN

TWENTY MINUTES LATER, Brad tucked his arm over my shoulder and steered me toward town. At 5'10", I was tall. Too tall for most guys to comfortably throw an arm over, but at 6'3", Brad had no trouble. It felt like an almost hug. Dusk settling in, the air was even colder than before, and it felt delightfully cozy to be next to someone so warm. I ran an arm around his waist and leaned my head into his shoulder. Snug as a bug in a rug.

"I wonder if I'd have made it as a ballerina like I'd dre ..." My stride hitched as I realized my thoughts had slipped into actual spoken words. Shit.

I pulled away from Brad. Evidently, I was feeling too cozy.

Brad smiled, tugging me back into his nook. I tensed for a second, then melted. *Damn.*

"Is it weird that part of me is glad I never got the chance to fail?" I asked. If I was sharing, I figured I might as well go all in. "I loved ballet so much; it's kind of nice to believe in the inevitability of something that can never be. To hold wholeheartedly to the belief, I would have succeeded as a ballerina if not for Perun."

Brad chuckled. "Baseball."

"Huh?"

"It's not weird. For me that was baseball. I broke my pitching arm in high school, and that ended my Major League dreams. Now I get to believe I would have made it if only my mom hadn't fishtailed on the ice and run us into a tree."

I was about to ask Brad more about baseball when the theater appeared. Like everything else in town, it was modern, the exterior an undulating wave of golden glass with shadowed images of ballerinas leaping across the waves, one after the other. The building was graceful movement like the dancers inside of it. "It's amazing," I whispered. "Are the images always playing?"

"I'm not sure actually, it only opened a few weeks ago. Hey M, before we get tickets, I need to talk to you about something."

Here it was. Brad wanted to talk about the call from the CIA. Part of me was surprised he wanted to broach it before Alexandra's extraction. With Albert injured, he needed my help, and if I flipped out on him like I'd done at the vet's office, he'd be up shit creek. I smiled, my eyes searching his. *Please don't lie to me. I'm so close to trusting you. Don't ruin it.* "Shoot," I said.

"I got a call from the CIA this afternoon, and it looks like …" Brad's voice was way too peppy. I closed my eyes. *Please don't lie.* "I'm going to need to go higher up the food chain for your immunity deal." My eyes flicked open as Brad's hand reached for my cheek then pulled away before touching me. His brow was crinkled with worry, his eyes sorrowful. "Please don't be upset. I still have strings to pull. We haven't lost yet."

"Thank you," I said, wrapping him in a fierce hug.

Brad pulled back, "You heard me, right? I didn't get the deal. Not yet."

"I heard you."

"Why are you so excited?"

"Because you could have lied and you didn't. That means everything."

"I'm going to keep trying."

"I know you will. Thank you," I said, knowing Brad's chances of brokering a deal for me were infinitesimal. People didn't just get immunity for good behavior; you needed something to trade, and after the CIA had our intel on Perun and Alexandra, I had nothing left. Still, it was the thought that counted.

"M?"

I cocked an eyebrow. "Brad?"

"I'll never lie to you. I promise."

"Okay," I said, trying to smile through my discomfort. Like 'I love you,' that was the kind of statement usually receiving a return of sentiment, which I couldn't give. From overhearing his conversation with the CIA, I knew Brad had already surmised my plan to withhold the names of the other cadets. While it was more an omission than a lie, it still wasn't truthful, and I couldn't promise to be truthful in the future either. Not if the other cadets were at stake. For them, I would lie to Brad until I was blue in the face. "You got Albert and Alexandra immunity, right?" I asked, wanting to redirect his attention.

Brad considered me for a moment then nodded. I smiled back, trying to look relaxed. I pointed to the box office. "Should we go ask about tickets?"

Brad checked his watch. "Yep. And we can grab dinner afterward. I know the best little Mom and Pop restaurant a couple of blocks from here. Real Olissan home cooking.

You'll love it. They have the best caramel and apple pie you'll ever taste."

"Them's fighting words," I laughed. "My mom was a mean cook."

Brad grinned, the sides of his eyes crinkling. "It's nice to hear you talk about her." He glanced at the queuing line. "I'll be back in a jiff."

I sat on the steps so I could watch the building. It was almost meditative the way movement flowed across from one side to the other. Like reading a book, it was a story. As Brad neared the front of the line, I crossed my fingers. I'd been iffy about coming, but now that I was here, I wanted to go. I wanted to close the chapter on ballet as a dream so that I could start a new one.

His turn, Brad pulled his wallet out. Everyone before him looked like they were picking up tickets already purchased. I held my breath as he spoke to the ticket agent. From my position, I couldn't see his face or hear him, but I knew when his body wilted that the ballet wasn't happening. Disappointed, I let my breath out. So much for bright ideas, at least we could still grab dinner.

I stood and smiled as Brad approached, looking like a dejected puppy. "It's okay."

Brad shook his head. "No, it's not. You stay there. I'll be right back."

"Where are you going?"

"I'll be right back," he said, darting across the street and disappearing around a corner.

Annoyed and cold, I sat down, scrunching into my coat. If there were no tickets, there were no tickets. There wasn't anything to be done.

Brad returned a few minutes later with a lightness to his step and a Machiavellian grin. "One sec," he said, jogging past me toward the box office. He pulled his wallet out again but didn't get in line, instead standing off to the side. Realizing what he was up to, I started to laugh. Not some half-laugh but a real honest to goodness belly shaker. Brad was a good friend. A *really* good one. I watched as he approached one couple with their ticket envelope in hand. He took out a wad of cash and gesticulated wildly with his hands, pointing at me sitting on the steps. The couple glanced my way then shook their heads no, weaving around him. Undaunted, Brad accosted another couple. He got a taker on the third attempt and came bouncing over with our tickets. He looked adorably happy with his broad smile and twinkling eyes. He helped me up and offered his arm. "Milady, tonight we see Romeo and Juliet by Prokofiev."

I tucked my arm under his and looked up into his eyes. I'd always thought of Brad as a good-looking man, but for the first time, I melted a little under the gaze of his emerald eyes. "From the bottom of my heart, thank you for this. Thank you for everything."

"It's my pleasure M. Truly."

# TWENTY-EIGHT

*Two Days Later*
*Istanbul, Turkey*

I SURVEYED THE room for the millionth time. I was in the grand ballroom of Büyük, the conference hotel, and had been for the last four hours. Alexandra would be taking the stage momentarily to close the morning session with her talk on cold fusion. Brad was seated at the rear of the ballroom by the exit doors, while Varos was in the front left corner, and I was in the front right. Judging by the buzz of conversation that flared up between each speaker, the conference was an exciting one, at least for those scientifically-minded. Eavesdropping on the conversations around me during the breaks, it seemed like the who's who of the alternative energy world was here. It was no wonder Alexandra wanted to give her speech before her extraction. Speaking here was a huge coup.

The ballroom erupted into a round of applause when the speaker on stage finished. "I can't believe they got Karl Leibowitz to come speak at this. He's such a rock star," said the Tom Hanks twin next to me as he clapped wildly.

Humbled by the applause, Karl put his hands together and bowed to the crowd before giving a final wave and gesturing to Alexandra as she wheeled in from a side door. The conference moderator stepped to the podium. "I'm very pleased to introduce the final speaker this morning, Dr. Alina Kasarian, a nuclear physicist, presenting today about her groundbreaking research in cold fusion. Following Dr. Kasarian's talk will be a short set of announcements and then lunch in the rotunda." He gestured toward Alexandra, "Without further ado."

Alexandra rolled onto the stage, and the moderator handed her a wireless mic and a clicker for the overhead projection screen, then grabbed the podium she was unable to stand at and carried it off the stage.

Alexandra smiled, her eyes scanning the crowd as everyone clapped. Despite my being in disguise, she was still able to find me. Her smile widened at the sight, and she visibly relaxed. Via the communication system Albert had set up with Alexandra, messages embedded in her research files, we'd been able to alert her to Albert's injuries and the switch to me running point on her extraction. Late in the game changes were never a good thing, but this mission was a GO.

"It's an honor to be speaking with you today about my research into cold fusion. You may well remember the work of Fleischmann and Pon, who were the first scientists who claimed to produce a cold fusion reaction. After the scientific community and governments worldwide did backflips over the idea of abundant clean energy, repeated attempts to reproduce the experiments failed. That disappointment led many to conclude cold fusion was not a theoretical possibility, but I'm here to tell you cold fusion is possible, and

I'm going to prove it to you!" Alexandra smiled bashfully at the crowd who sat in rapt attention. "The physicists among you are probably saying that's not possible. That I'm cheating or have made a miscalculation, but I can assure you, that is not the case!" Alexandra shrugged, offering another smile, the crowd eating up her tongue-in-cheek arrogance. It was a brilliant ploy on her part. While arrogance among men is accepted, among women it will easily get you labeled as a bitch, unless you soften the blow to the male ego with a little bit of charm. Yep, Alexandra was a smartie.

"While nuclear reactors have the capacity to supply huge amounts of energy to the masses, they also come with unparalleled dangers. One only has to look at the reactor meltdowns in Tokaimura, Chernobyl and Three Mile Island. With the world's population growing and energy demands increasing at an exponential rate, some would like us to believe nuclear energy is the solution to our energy problem. As I'm talking to a room full of leaders in alternative energies, I'm sure you'd beg to disagree. The risks are too high, and we need another solution. I regret to inform you that you're about to be out of a job as cold fusion is that solution. Alexandra laughed sweetly, her playful eyes washing over the crowd. Some of the crowd laughed with her, but many didn't.

"No. Seriously," she said. "Alternative energies like solar and thermal offer only a stop-gap solution to the energy crisis. Cold fusion, on the other hand, is not one of the many solutions to the world's energy problems. It is *the* solution. The ability to split the atom under cold, safe conditions means limitless energy for the world. With cold fusion comes the capacity to change the lives of the world's impoverished by supplying them with low-cost electricity. There will be no need for coal or petroleum, two of the biggest contributors to poor air quality. There will be no need for deep sea oil drilling or freighters full of petroleum. Oil spills will be a thing of the past. Hydroelectric dams can be removed, returning our waterways to a natural state."

Pausing to let her words sink in, Alexandra eyed the crowd, which was now a sea of murmurs, some were whispering in appreciation, others in disdain, probably depending on whether they were a true tree hugger or a closet capitalist. Although her words excited me, they also left a sour taste in my mouth and a pit in my stomach. Alexandra's superior attitude toward the crowd, although perhaps deserved, was not exactly friendly, and I wasn't sure how Albert would take to it. I certainly hoped she wouldn't treat him like she was treating her audience.

"I've got a treat for you today," said Alexandra, continuing. "Some of you are probably thinking although I may have unlocked the physics of cold fusion, technology employing it will still be years away. You think you still have time to make your money and build your empire, but that's not the case. Cold fusion technology is ready now." Alexandra nodded to one of her bodyguards who walked onto the stage, carrying a small cylindrical device. "Inside this case is a cold fusion cell and enough energy to power the entire city of Istanbul for several months. Don't believe me, take a look at my test video." Alexandra turned to the screen behind her and used her clicker. A video appeared that showed the same device integrated into a larger system I couldn't decipher the function of. "This is the power station for Ulan, Olissa's capital city. Last week, there was a momentary citywide blackout as the station stopped drawing power from the Krator hydroelectric dam and began drawing from this single cold fusion power cell. Power has been stable and uninterrupted since that day." Alexandra raised her hands to the sky. "It's the dawn of a new age," she said, finding my eyes and smiling.

I couldn't quite bring myself to smile, but I nodded and clapped because what else can you do when told about world-saving technology. The rest of the audience seemed to agree because they also joined in the applause, hesitant at first, but then with vigor as the exhilaration of being present at such an historic event began to grip people. This was the Berlin Wall coming down. This was V-E Day.

As everyone clapped, I couldn't help but think *thank God. Thank God Perun won't be able to use this technology to cripple the world. No one will know how close things came to being catastrophically bad.*

# TWENTY-NINE

ALEXANDRA BOWED HER head to the crowd, which now hooted and hollered like she was the second coming of Einstein, and maybe she was. When she lifted her head, her eyes met mine. She smiled broadly and nodded then turned to the crowd and waved. This was her time to shine, and I was happy to let her revel in it. If she wanted to, she could continue her research back in the States, but public appearances would be out of the question. Defecting agents from foreign countries needed to keep a low profile. The intelligence community liked to keep the ins and outs of their spy world dealings from the general public. Sure real stuff leaked out in books and movies, but if it was sold as fiction, there was no real harm. The public thought of it as espionage fantasy.

The crowd was still cheering as Alexandra turned her chair and began to roll toward the stage ramp. She stopped at the top and waved one last time, smiling and laughing. The sweet and bashful girl from the beginning of the talk was back, and I wished Albert was here to see it. His granddaughter, the star. Although I'd found myself jealous of

Alexandra more often than not, listening to the applause, all I felt was hopeful and maybe a little proud. I knew this girl. I was helping this amazing woman reunite with her family. Despite her reservations, Alexandra had come through for us. For me. Because of her, Perun would be decimated, and I would be closer to having my freedom.

Alexandra glided down the ramp and was met by two of her bodyguards. Two more were beyond the door, and another guard floated in the crowd. I got up quickly as she exited the auditorium. We wanted Alexandra down the hall and out of the way before things got crowded outside during lunch. She wasn't as mobile as a normal extractee, or as easy to hide.

The plan was to meet Alexandra in the conference room by the West exit where we had a getaway van parked outside. Varos would take care of her floating guard while Brad was in charge of the two outside. The two guards flanking her fell to me. Her team of five guards was connected via mic. Varos had already identified their transmission frequency and was ready to jam it as soon as the first guard went down so the others couldn't be warned. It was standard procedure for the guards to be in regular contact, and Alexandra's flanking guards would be on alert when they lost contact with the others, but would not yet go to full lock down. That's where I came in. As I exited the auditorium, I ditched my glasses and shrugged on a black jacket with the hotel logo then gathered my hair into a ponytail, spinning it into an efficient bun. Now, I was someone who didn't seem out of place anywhere in the hotel. This didn't mean her guards wouldn't be suspicious of me, but it did mean they'd hesitate. I was just staff. Just a girl. Being a girl would buy me an extra second or two, which was why I scored point on the mission. Spying was the only job where sexist attitudes were a plus for a woman.

Big, brawny guys didn't like to think a girl would ever be sent to take them out. The mere thought was insulting.

I spotted Alexandra wheeling toward the far hall and our exit point and picked up my pace. The mic crackled in my ear. "Targets contained. Varos report?" said Brad. In my peripheral vision, I saw Brad coming out of a storage room, his suit jacket ruffled. Varos' mic crackled to life. "Could use some …"

I slowed for a second, glancing at Brad. He was already heading for the East exit and Varos. For all that muscles had replaced his flab, Varos was never a very coordinated fighter. We knew going in; he might have trouble.

I picked up speed again only to halt a second later. Alexandra was stopped at the hallway's edge glancing back my way. What was she doing?

Was she panicking? Having second thoughts? Her face was blank. Unreadable. She had to go down the hall to the extraction point. I couldn't help her here. People would be filing out of the auditorium any second. I smiled and nodded her forward. *You'll be fine. Go on. Stick to the plan. Albert's waiting to meet you.*

As if she was seeing through me, Alexandra nodded with a passing smile then turned back down the hall.

I breathed a sigh of relief and started walking. *Thank the L—*

Someone grabbed me from behind, yanking me into an empty conference room. He pulled the gun stowed at my back and tossed it to the floor. We'd been found out but how? My dad? Another man followed us inside the room. Having no leverage to push forward and throw off the man holding me, I stomped down on his toes with my boot and slammed my head back catching him in the jaw. He careened backward taking me with him. We landed in a heap, and

I rolled off to the side, slamming my elbow down onto his nose. He howled and curled in on himself. I was grabbing for his gun when … BOOM!

The shock wave hit, flattening me. I must have blacked out for a few seconds because I woke to a haze of dust dancing over my head. My ears rang and when I tried to sit, my head spun. I turned to puke, and my stomach contents landed on a finger. No hand, no body, just a finger. I recoiled and scrambled away. I fell a couple of times, once onto a folding table and then onto a chair. At some point, I finally started to hear things—cries, screams, the crack of falling debris. My fingers fumbled for the earbud. "Milena reporting. Is everyone okay? I'm going for Alexandra now."

I didn't wait for a reply. I grabbed my gun and exited, trying to piece things together. My equilibrium returning, I broke into a jog.

# THIRTY

A SECOND BLAST shook the hotel as I raced down the hall, then a third. Plaster rained from the ceiling and far away screams echoed down the hall. This side of the building seemed stable, at least so far. I could only hope there wouldn't be a fourth and fifth blast.

Alexandra was headed toward a room by the West exit before they grabbed me. With the blasts, her guards would have made a beeline for that door. Taking out Alexandra's guard detail was riskier outside, but hopefully, pedestrians nearby would be too engrossed in the smoke billowing out of the hotel to notice anything amiss.

Careening around the corner, I saw the exit and picked up my pace as another wave of adrenaline hit. Albert had entrusted me to bring his granddaughter home, and I was not going to let him down. Running past the room where I was to meet Alexandra, I glanced inside just in case she had somehow talked her guards into staying within the building. I thought the chances of seeing her inside were nil, but there she was, sitting by herself in the middle of the room, her hands folded and her face calm.

I skidded to a stop as her eyes flicked to mine.

We stared at each other across an expanse.

She was there, right where I asked her to be but …

On guard, I took a hesitant step forward, something niggling at me. Why was Alexandra so calm? Bombs were going off, why wasn't …

Shouldn't she …

My stomach plummeted, and bile scorched up my throat.

She wouldn't …

She couldn't have …

But why would …

What about Albert and …

I stepped through the door, my gun drawn and ready to clear the blind corners I couldn't yet see. I caught flashes of movement from my left and right. Alexandra wasn't alone in the room. There were two men, one in each corner. Waiting. Within that millisecond, I knew all that I needed to. Alexandra was not on my side.

I swung my gun to my right and fired as I kicked out with my left leg. The man on my right went down while the one on my left staggered back, scrambling to regain control of the gun bobbling in his hands. I had a second before he would regain control, and I used it to my advantage, turning my gun on him.

Two shots rang out. One hit my target, who crumpled.

The other, Alexandra's shot, hit me, bulleting through the shoulder on my already bad arm. Knocked off balance, I stumbled backward into a wall. Shot up with adrenaline; I felt a blast of pain I knew would get far worse later if there was a later. I put Alexandra in my gun sight. She should have kept firing until she'd downed me but hadn't. Rookie mistake.

I fired, hitting her in the arm.

She dropped the gun, howling in pain. How had I not seen this coming? And why was she still in the hotel? Was she waiting to see if I survived the blast? Did she want to make sure I died?

"Why?" I asked. "Why turn away from Albert?"

Clutching her bleeding arm, Alexandra glared. "Vladik's my family. Perun's my family. Not Albert Gastone."

"Perun's no one's family. They don't care about us. They don't care about you."

Alexandra started to laugh. "Maybe not you, but they care about me. You were a pawn on their front lines. A piece to be sacrificed. I'm their queen."

"They tried to kill you," I said, unable to hide my disdain.

"It was a mistake on their part. They didn't yet realize who I was, and what I could do. Cold fusion will change the world. My work and I are everything to Perun. Everything to Vladik."

"If cold fusion is everything you say then why blow up the competition?" I asked, gesturing out the door.

"They were needless barriers we would have overcome, but why should I wait when I have the answer?"

"But you just killed people. Some of the world's brightest minds."

Alexandra cackled. "I'm the world's brightest mind. I'm Einstein and Oppenheimer."

I stared at Alexandra in disbelief. She was certifiable. Just as Perun had used my mother to indoctrinate me, they'd played upon Alexandra's brilliance to indoctrinate her. Now she was so buoyed by delusions of grandeur; she couldn't see reason.

"So what, you wanted to take out Albert along with all your competition? Why? All he wanted to do was help you. You could have said no."

Alexandra smirked as she dug at something in her pocket. My old … her old locket appeared. She threw it at me, and it landed several feet short, like a worthless outgrown token. "I could have told him no? Hardly. He would have meddled and made himself a nuisance. It was best that he go down with the rest. It's too bad he couldn't make it today."

My anger surging, I lunged forward and pistol-whipped Alexandra across the face. "How dare you. Albert is a great man."

"Vladik's a great man. I'm a great woman. We're a great team. Albert is nothing, and neither are you," she spat, pushing up with her arms and nailing me with a head butt that sent me reeling backward. She grabbed onto my shirt as I fell, and my momentum took us both to the floor in a tangled heap.

She reached for my gun with one hand while seizing my throat with the other, putting her full body weight behind it. With the dead weight of her lower half, she was surprisingly heavy for a small person, and I couldn't get any leverage to throw her off. With my free hand, I slammed into the arm pressing into my throat multiple times, but it wouldn't budge. I saw stars. Knowing if I passed out, I wouldn't be waking up, I switched tactics from trying to dislodge the hand at my throat to breaking my gun hand free. I jerked my arm up and down, but still her hand stayed attached to mine. Damn, the girl was strong. Blackness creeping in on me now, I did the only thing I could think of and slowly relaxed, stopping my fight. Going, going …

Alexandra held firm for one second, two. She growled, pressing harder. Three. Four. Five. I was a second from going under for good when her grip finally lessened.

In that instant, I jerked my gun hand out from under hers and fired.

# THIRTY-ONE

I CLOSED MY eyes as I pushed Alexandra's dead weight off me and to the side. I gasped for breaths. After being strangled, I needed air desperately, but my throat constricted as my emotions took control and my eyes flooded. I opened my mouth willing the air to come, but my body was working against me. I choked on each inhale barely getting anything inside my lungs. I felt like I was strangling myself.

"M?" said a voice. "Oh my God, are you alright?"

"Can't. Breathe," I choked.

Brad looked at Alexandra beside me and the gun in my hand then glanced behind him at the two men near the door.

A torrent of tears claimed me as he surveyed the scene. Nothing would ever be right in the world again, at least not in my world. I'd killed Albert's granddaughter. Seeing the gold of Alexandra's discarded locket, I peeled myself off the floor, and crawled toward it, still struggling to take in air. Snatching it, I clutched it to my chest. The locket may have started out hers, but it was meant to be mine. I was the one who appreciated it. I was the one who respected what it signified. *How could Alexandra have let her past mean so little?*

"Come on. Let's get you up." Brad took my arms and pulled me upright. "Just breathe."

Exiting the hotel, we stumbled across the street and slumped down together against a tree in the park. The ground was soggy from last night's rain, but I barely noticed. Plumes of black smoke still billowed from the hotel. Sirens blared as fire engines and ambulances arrived. Like us, survivors were staggering their way outside. They were covered in dirt and blood and had that vacant, hollow look you see in news footage after a catastrophe. I still struggled to find a normal breathing rhythm. I'd get two greedy breaths, and it would hitch, and I'd have to struggle past it for another breath.

"What happened?" asked Brad, breaking our silence a few minutes later.

"Varos?" I asked.

Brad shook his head. "He's not responding to comms but—" Brad must have seen my face begin to contort because he put a hand on my shoulder. "M. Hold it together. There are a million reasons Varos might not be responding. Can you tell me what happened with Alexandra?"

I didn't immediately reply. In fact, I don't think I spoke for several minutes. The only sound was my breathing. Varos wasn't answering coms and was probably dead along with Alexandra.

Alexandra, who I killed.

How would I ever look Albert in the eyes again? Would Albert even believe me about Alexandra being our enemy?

I thought of Albert waiting for us, alive but frail. He'd almost died because of what I brought into his life. Because of what Alexandra and I brought in. Now I was going to have to tell him she'd gone bad, that he'd lost her twice. People could only stand to lose so much before they became a shell with nothing left inside. Would this break him? Would he even believe me?

I pulled away and turned so I could see Brad's face. My stomach was clenched in such a tight knot it felt worse than the bullet to my shoulder, which was starting to whine. Would Brad believe me? Or would he think I'd acted out of jealousy? I found his eyes. "Alexandra and Vladik were working together. She was never with us. The files she sent will be worthless. She knew about the bombs. I shot her. Killed her. She was going to kill me."

I studied Brad's face. The only thing registering was surprise, but I couldn't tell whether it was surprise over Alexandra's actions or mine. I reached out and took Brad's hand. "You know I love Albert. I would never take her from him, not if I didn't have to. Please tell me you believe me."

Brad started to nod. Such an ambiguous gesture, the nod. It means 'yes' but yes to what. He looked past me to the broken hotel. "The world has lost some of the greatest minds in alternative energy ..." His eyes pulled focus and returned to me. "They did this, didn't they? Alexandra and Vladik? To eliminate the competition."

I nodded. "You believe me then?"

Brad's eyebrows screwed up. "Of course, I believe you. I know you. For better or worse. I know you were jealous of Alexandra but tried not to be. I know you love Albert and would never hurt him on purpose." Brad paused, leaning in until his face was only inches from mine. "I know you brought Varos in to help keep the names and locations of the other cadets from me and the CIA."

"Why did you still try to get me a deal?"

Brad shrugged. "Because I know you. I know what you will and won't do. You're loyal. Before Albert, the cadets were your family. You wouldn't betray them knowingly. Not if you didn't have to. You're a good person, M. You might not look that way on paper to the CIA, but I know you are. And I'm going to keep trying to get you that ..." Brad's eyes wandered from mine, and his mouth broke into a huge smile. "I never thought I'd say this but happy to see you, man."

I whipped around and stumbled to my feet. Varos stood ten feet away, bloody but mostly unharmed. "We've been trying to reach you on comms," I said, wrapping him in a hug. "I thought you were dead."

"No such luck," said Varos, squeezing me tight. "I got stuck behind a fallen piece of ceiling in the East Corridor for a while, and my earbud got toasted in the blast." Varos glanced at Brad. "Mind if I borrow O for a minute?"

"You're bothering to ask?"

Varos laughed. "Good point. The blast must have knocked a screw loose."

I followed Varos. "Turns out Alexandra wasn't on our side," I said, thinking Varos wanted a debrief on the mission. "Can I fill you in on the ins and outs later? I'm still—"

"I don't need to know," he said, shaking his head. "I'm getting out of here before the CIA comes down on our heads, and you need to do the same. There's no immunity deal for you, and I know there isn't one for me, so we need to disappear." From his jacket pocket, Varos produced an envelope-sized package. "I've got you a new identity and a credit card. I'm headed to Zanzibar where I plan to disappear for a good long time. You're welcome to join me or go off on your own."

"Varos, I—"

He put a finger to my lips. "I don't know if there's anything beyond friendship between us. I think maybe there is, but even if there isn't, we are friends above all. If you decide to come, we can look out for each other." He leaned in and his lips found mine for the briefest of caresses. Both of us were battered and bruised, covered in blood and soot, yet that kiss spoke of possibilities.

"I have something I need to take care of before I go anywhere with anyone," I said, smiling sadly.

Varos shook his head. "Don't do it, O. Leave it behind you. It's not our mess."

"You're wrong. My family. My mess. I killed Mistress. My father will want to find me, and if I'm not there to be found, he might come after someone I love."

Varos studied me, his hands clenching and unclenching. "Two graves."

"What?"

"That's what they say about revenge. Dig two graves."

"That's a stupid saying, and this isn't revenge. It's insurance. I want to be free of all this, but I can't do that if I'm always looking over my shoulder. It's time my dad and I played our last game."

Varos leaned in until his forehead touched mine. "Please, don't get yourself killed."

I smiled. "Don't plan to."

"So I guess, I'll maybe see you soon?"

"Yep."

"All right then."

"All right."

With a weary sigh, Varos pulled away. He made it all of two steps before I grabbed his arm and pulled him back. I didn't know what my plans were or even if I could best my dad, but if this was the last we'd see of each other, I wanted our parting to be better than this. My emotions getting the best of me, I grabbed him in a fierce hug. Varos chortled, his body shaking, but he complied, wrapping one hand around my back and smoothing my hair with the other. "I love you," I said, nuzzling into his neck and breathing him in. There was only a hint of his normal smell amid the odor of blood and fire, but I savored it. The same height, our faces touched as we hugged and when a wash of need came over me, I realized I wanted more than a hug. I softly kissed his jaw, his cheek, and then finding his lips, I kissed those too. The kiss was a goodbye. A hello. A maybe. One thing was for sure, though; it was a kiss to remember. No matter what, we'd always have the kiss.

When it ended, Varos smiled, bopped me on the nose and departed without another word.

I glanced back at Brad and found him furtively looking my way. "I guess your stalking ways die hard," I said, walking over.

"I was worried you two might run away together and leave me to tell Albert about Alexandra."

"I'm not a coward."

"I know that. I just—"

"I'm done lying."

Brad reached out an arm and tugged me into a hug. "I know that, too."

"You'll help me, though? I don't know if I can do it alone. He might not believe me."

Brad ran a hand through my hair. "He'll believe you. I know he will. But we're a team, and we'll do this together. I wasn't lying when I said I'd always have your back."

I looked up into Brad's beautiful green eyes. They were gorgeous. He was gorgeous. "I know that now," I whispered.

# THIRTY-TWO

BRAD AND I made record time getting to Bursa, which was both good and bad. Albert couldn't participate in the op but wanted to meet us right after. Taking Alexandra back to the country we were helping her defect from was out of the question, so Sam agreed to drive Albert from Olissa to Bursa, a major sea port near Istanbul. The plan had been to meet Albert there, and hop a freighter to Greece where we could catch a flight to anywhere. The whole drive to Bursa, I felt like we were speeding toward my doom.

At the hotel, I was a death row inmate walking to the electric chair, as I inched down the hall toward Albert's room. My stomach fought to purge itself of food that wasn't even there. I hadn't eaten. I couldn't. I would have stalled if not for Brad holding my hand. On the drive, I'd gone through a hundred ways to word the news, trying to find the most painless one, the least jarring. Did *gone* or *passed* sound better than *dead*? What about *Perun turned her*? Was that better or worse than *she was loyal to Perun*? I fumbled the room's keycard as we neared, and Brad bent down to pick it up. Seeing my terror, he put a hand on my shoulder and nudged up my chin, so our eyes met. "This is not on you. We're doing this together. Albert will survive this and so will you."

"What if he doesn't believe me?" I asked, my voice cracking.

"You don't think anyone knows you, but *we* do. There is no doubt in my mind that he'll believe you. No doubt whatsoever."

A door creaked opened, and Albert appeared in the hall. For a split second, there was a relieved smile on his face until he saw that there were two, not three of us. He studied us, his eyes drifting one to the other, taking in our grim demeanors. "I'm so sorry, Albert. Alexandra wasn't on our side," I said, gripping Brad's arm for support.

"Sh-She … wasn't?" he asked, throwing his hand out to the wall for support as his body went slack.

I shook my head. "It's Perun's fault. You have no idea how strong their indoctrination measures are. I'm so sorry."

He stumbled toward me, taking me in a hug. "How'd it happen?"

I wanted to hold tight to Albert, desperate to keep him as my own, but with his injuries, I didn't want to hurt him. "She came at me …" My voice shook. "She tried to kill me so …"

Albert began to shake, and he pulled me even closer. Brad put a reassuring hand on each of our shoulders. I looked into Brad's eyes and found them welling with tears. He nodded me on. I needed to say the words. If Albert and I were ever going to heal, the words needed to be spoken aloud. "I … killed … her, Albert," I choked, my voice catching on every word. "I killed her."

Albert gulped in a breath, sobbing now, but still he held me. "I'm so sorry," he whispered. "I'm so sorry. Please forgive me."

I pulled back, holding Albert's shoulders. "Forgive you? What's there to forgive?"

"I should have never let you get involved. When I realized who you were, I should have taken you somewhere far away and not let you play this spy game. You almost got killed because of me. I would have never forgiven myself."

"Wow, we should be Catholic," I laughed, relief flooding me. "The guilt runs deep with us. I love you, Albert. More than you can know."

"I love you, too, Milena. I love you, too."

# THIRTY-THREE

*If you know the enemy and know yourself, you need not fear the result of a hundred battles. If you know yourself but not the enemy, for every victory gained you will also suffer a defeat. If you know neither the enemy nor yourself, you will succumb in every battle.*

Sun Tzu, *The Art of War*

I CUPPED THE mug between my hands missing the warmth of the coffee I'd drained. Outside the diner window, a scattering of snowflakes twirled and danced in the wind before settling on the pavement and parked cars.

Always aware of her customers, Elena, the waitress, appeared with another two mugs. "Thanks," I said, as she set one by me and the other opposite. She retrieved my empty mug and the full one that had gone cold.

Elena nodded. "Do you think whoever you're waiting for will show up today?"

"Maybe. Or maybe tomorrow," I said, reaching across and arranging the coffee cup handle so that it would suit my father, a lefty.

"We have some magazines behind the counter if you're bored," she offered, surveying the empty table. It was my fourth day at the diner, and so far, all I'd done was drink coffee, pick at a grilled cheese for lunch, drink more coffee, and then close out my day by picking at a piece of pie. I didn't read or surf the net. Instead, I watched the window and the diner's rear door while fingering the radio tracker my dad had implanted. They were my focus until closing each day and would be until my dad picked up my signal and came for a chat. I knew he'd be looking for me. I'd killed Mistress and Father would want his revenge.

"I'm fine but thank you. I have a lot to think about."

I turned my gaze back to the window. For the last four days, I'd been going over my plan. Reviewing everything I knew about my father. I was taking a risk by sitting in the diner with every booth and table visible through the windows. Dear old dad could easily snuff me with a sniper rifle and call it a day, or try and grab me as I left each night. But if I'd judged my dad correctly, he'd want to talk with me first. Educate me. Point out my lack of skill as a chess player. Zakhar Rokva was an arrogant man, and I planned to play that to my advantage, if he didn't shoot me in the head first, that is.

It was mid-afternoon when I spotted my dad ambling across the parking lot, the picture of nonchalance. The tension I'd held for the last four days increased tenfold at the sight of him. He was right where I wanted him … in my crosshairs. And he didn't even know it. Part of me wanted to rebel at thinking in such a calculated manner, about my father no less, but another part craved the honey sweet taste of freedom. The leash holding my old life needed to be cut, and Father was its last thread.

*You can do this.*

*You will do this.*

A bell over the door rang as Father entered. He stopped to scan his surroundings, and Elena approached him with a menu. He bustled past her without acknowledgment and slid into the seat opposite me, wrapping his hands around the steaming mug of coffee in front of him.

"You been waiting long?" he asked.

"Four days. I'm sitting in an American-style diner in the center of the city. What took you so long?"

Zakhar laughed, but it held no humor. "I've been busy with clean up."

My stomach dipped. My throat constricted. "There's a bit of a mess, isn't there?"

Father shook his head. "You have no idea what you've done. To this country. To me."

"You don't give me enough credit."

"I think I gave you too much credit. That was my folly."

I stared into my father's eyes, looking for any hint the man I'd once known was still somewhere in there. "Did Mistress kill Mother?"

"Probably."

"Probably? You don't know?"

"In all likelihood, yes. Mistress wanted you back, and Sibel wouldn't let you go and threatened to expose Mistress." Zakhar chuckled. "That woman was a spitfire. She didn't fully understand what Mistress and I were up to, but she knew just enough to get her in trouble."

"The day you dropped me at Perun, you said it was me or one of the boys. Why, if I was the one she wanted?"

"Believe it or not, I loved Sibel. When she died, I wanted to keep you, but Mistress threatened to hurt your brothers. It was you or them."

My face puckered as if I'd eaten something sour. "How

could you *be* with Mistress. Mom was a saint and Mistress was—"

"The love of my life," said Father. "I loved Sibel for her purity and Ekaterina for her passion to the cause. Our work for Perun was important and necessary for Olissa to be strong."

I sucked in a breath, a chill racing down my spine. "Perun used a bunch of kids as sacrificial lambs. They stole our lives."

"Perun gave your lives purpose. The cause was worthy and just until … it wasn't. Vladik ruined it all. Mistress and I are patriots."

"Don't you mean 'were' patriots? The devil incarnate is dead."

The corner of Dad's mouth quirked. "If she's the devil incarnate then what does that make you?"

My eyes widened in horror, a horror that quickly turned to anger and then back to horror again. I wasn't twisted and warped like Mistress, but I also wasn't good. I had killed people. I was hoping to kill my father. There was a darkness in me, a capacity to snuff life in an instant when others might pause or resist. "That would make me the devil's spawn," I said, trying to make my voice strong. "Are you afraid?"

"Not in the least," said Zakhar, raising the coffee cup to his lips.

My heart stalled as he took a sip, then recovered, racing forward. *One man's terrorist is another's freedom fighter.* "You should be. You did shoot my dog, tag me with a radio tracker and almost kill Albert. You're not exactly sitting pretty in my eyes."

Father shook his head, his eyes going skyward. *Poor little delusional Milena.* "You've never bested me before, what makes you think you will this time?"

"I killed Mistress. I helped bring down Perun. I think I may be winning this game." The deed was now done. I'd won our game as soon as my father took a sip of poisoned coffee. Now all that was left to do was try to understand how we, a father and a daughter who had once loved each other, came to sit at this table; each prepared to kill the other. "So why the tracker? Did you want me to get Vladik for you only to get pissed when you realized you'd also led me to your boss, Tarkan? Sorry about figuring that one out."

Father took another careful sip of his coffee then set it on the table, the corners of his mouth creeping up. "That was a larger game with other players. This is us playing one-on-one. It's chess. And you've never beaten me. I play five moves ahead, and you play three. You'll never win."

I leaned forward and casually tapped the rim of his coffee cup. "You're right. You probably would beat me at chess given it's a barbarian's game with simple head-on battles. It's all about total victory or defeat. It's a game for men like you with all its narrow rules. Times have changed, Dad. You need to adapt or you die."

Father appraised me, his brow furrowing. *Why didn't I seem more worried?*

I held his gaze. "Do you know how to beat someone at chess who's better than you?"

"You can't beat them," spat Father.

"Your veneer of confidence is beginning to crack. I see some worry in your eyes."

"You can't beat them," he said again, clamping his calm façade back into place. He snagged his coffee mug and leaned back in his seat, taking another sip. Recognizing a slight tremble in his hand, Father quickly returned the mug to the table and darted his hand away.

"You feeling it yet?" I asked, wiping away a renegade tear

that had fought its way free.

"Feel what?" he said, teeth gritted.

"Fatherly pride for my victory?" I whispered, choking down a sob.

"Quit talking nonsense," said Father, standing. His face blanched, and he wobbled before folding back down into the booth. He grabbed the coffee cup. "You didn't?"

My tears could no longer be contained and rained down my face in droves. "Do you want to know how to win a game of chess against someone who's better than you?"

Father's head cocked to the side, and his eyes softened. He reached out a shaking hand. *To wipe my tears?* "How?"

"You stop the game before it starts. Mom was right. Chess is a dumb game. I'd rather live life than play at war."

"I'm your father," he said, glancing at his coffee mug and pulling back the hand he'd extended. He tugged his shirt collar loose.

"I know. I took your advice and decided not to let my personal relationships get in my way. I still remember how you used to be, and I'll keep those good memories with me, but you're far too dangerous to let live."

"Killing me will change you, Milena. Forever."

I laughed, my anger surging. "You shot my dog and almost got Albert killed. You tried to take me out that day in the warehouse. You sent me to Perun and made me into this, someone who can kill. Why are you acting so shocked? It's okay for you to seek revenge, but I'm not allowed to protect myself? Protect my future?" I shook my head. "You were always so willing to school me on my weaknesses, let me school you on yours. You're arrogant. You think I still see you as my father. You think I still want your love. I tried to kill you that day outside Amalya's, yet you were still arrogant enough to come inside this diner and sit across from me like

I'm harmless. You drank coffee that you didn't order, coffee that I had ample opportunity to spike with poison. I may have been the one to put poison in your mug, but I didn't kill you. Your arrogance did that."

"Killing me will change you," he said again.

"I know it will, dad. I know it will. It's a price I'm willing to pay, but you're the last. I'm done being a spy. There will be no more deaths at my hand." I fished in my purse for some money and laid it on the table. "I loved you, Father. I'm sorry for this. The poison will be quick. Painless."

I stood, looking out the window as I shrugged on my coat. The dancing snowflakes were gone, replaced by icy bullets of sleet. A nice beach somewhere off the beaten path sounded pretty damn good. I glanced at Father one last time. I'm not sure why. It wasn't to revel in my hard won freedom or to mourn his loss. Maybe it was to see if now, in his final minutes, the Father I'd once known had returned. Wasn't your life supposed to flash before your eyes? Weren't there supposed to be epiphanies? Shouldn't my father see the error in his ways? Or at least recall the love of his family?

Father looked away, unwilling to meet my gaze. The man that had haunted my nightmares was now acting the coward. I would have never imagined it, but there it was. At Compound Perun, they'd taught us that spies handle the notion of death in two ways. By believing in their immortality or by embracing death as an inevitable fate to be met with honor. We were taught to embrace death, but I could see in Father's eyes he had clung to immortality.

Until now.

I almost felt sorry for him. Almost.

# THIRTY-FOUR

SEATED AT THE airport bar, I stared with disbelieving eyes at the TV screen. With tears streaking down his face, Vladik Kasarian spoke to reporters outside Pretor Cathedral, where Alina/Alexandra's memorial service would take place in an hour's time. My stomach churned as I knocked back my drink and asked for another. I wondered if Albert was watching. Hell, maybe he was there with the crowd of mourners. I liked that idea. It would be good for him to be surrounded by others. Maybe it would lessen his pain.

He'd fought for her when he thought she was dead. He'd fought to free her when he learned she was alive. And now she was dead … for real … by my hand. It didn't matter that she'd been corrupted. It was the loss of what could have been—the Alexandra he believed her to be—that Albert felt and mourned. The entirety of me ached at the thought. It wasn't fair. Not that she was dead. Not that I'd killed her. Not that Albert was mourning someone who never really existed. It wasn't fucking fair. I kicked back my second drink and ordered a third. When it arrived, I threw it back too. I was starting to get buzzed, and I liked it, wanting more. I wanted to drown.

The bartender set the fourth drink in front of me, but when I went to grab the glass, a hand clamped down on top, sliding it away. "You're cut off."

I whipped my head toward the voice and found Brad sliding onto the stool next to me. Oh Joy!

"I've been looking everywhere for you."

"Well, you found me."

Brad signaled to the bartender for a drink. "You're just leaving?"

I stared at the TV screen. "I am."

"What about Albert? He needs you."

"Is Albert's immunity deal still good even without Alexandra?"

"Yes, but—"

"He should go home then. Orkney needs him."

"He needs you."

I shook my head. "Trust me when I say no one needs to be around me right now. I'm seriously fucked up." I glanced at Brad then away. "I killed my father yesterday."

Brad reached a hand out and smoothed down my hair. "I'm sorry M."

"Me too."

"Are you planning to meet up with Varos?"

"Maybe. Not sure yet."

Brad studied me and my skin lit up under his gaze, but I wouldn't turn to face him. He was here to talk me out of leaving, and I needed to go. If I was going to survive this, I needed to walk away. Finally, Brad shifted his focus to the TV.

"Vladik's not dead," I noted, watching Kasarian tuck an arm around his very pregnant wife and lead her into the church. Tarkan was dead but not Vladik. One of the men responsible for all the despicable things Perun had done to me, the cadets, the world, was walking around free. "The CIA made a deal with him, didn't they?" I asked, my teeth gritted. "They made a deal with him but not me. Did he offer them cold fusion?"

"They did offer him a deal, unfortunately, but no, he didn't offer them cold fusion. That they took from the power substation Alexandra mentioned in her conference talk. The power cell is already being reverse engineered, as we speak." Brad's hand reached across and took mine. "I'm sorry, M. I'm really sorry."

I closed my eyes at the cool of Brad's hand. It was calming, but I didn't want to be calmed. I wanted to be pissed. I deserved to be pissed, Goddamnit. I pulled my hand out from underneath his and hid it under my leg.

"M, Vladik will be monitored and kept in line. Olissa will be stable. She'll continue to thrive."

My eyes breathed fire as I turned to face him, my blood boiled. "He deserves to be dead," I hissed, my body beginning to shake with an instantaneous, barely controlled rage. I wrenched my glass back from Brad and drained the liquid, basking in the burn as it snaked down my throat.

Brad put a hand on my shoulder and there was its calming cool again.

I shrugged it off.

He moved to my leg.

I brushed it away. "Stop," I glared. "Just stop."

I turned back to the TV, hoping he would leave if I ignored him.

My eyes bored into the screen, but I saw nothing.

"Milena," said Brad. "Milena."

I stared at the screen.

"Milena. Albert needs you. Don't leave."

Out of nowhere, a white-hot pain embraced the whole of my hand. I closed my eyes, sighing at the relief of it.

"Oh shit," said Brad, grabbing my arm and yanking my body around to face him. "Get me a towel."

*A towel? What?* I opened my eyes to find Brad staring at me, panicked. A towel appeared and Brad cradled my hand with it. The glass I held was now in pieces.

"The airport has a doctor on staff," said the barkeep. "I'll call him."

"No," I said, removing a shard. "I'm fine. Sorry about your glass. I'll pay for it."

The bartender picked up an identical glass, studying it. "Are you sure you're okay? I've never seen that happen before. It just shattered in your hand."

"Can we get a bucket of warm water?" asked Brad. The bartender nodded and disappeared into the back. "M, are you okay?"

I looked from my bloodied hand to Brad. "I can't stay," I whispered. "I can't watch him mourn someone who I killed. I need time. Time to figure stuff out. I don't know who I am anymore."

The bartender arrived with the bucket, and ushered us to an out-of-the-way corner where I wouldn't scare his other patrons. Brad put the bucket between his legs, then sank my hand into it. "All the visible pieces are out, your own bleeding and the water will help flush the rest." For a moment we both sat silently, watching the water as it swirled with blood. I wondered if there would ever be a day when I didn't hate the color red. "I'll make you a deal..."

I arched an eyebrow. "A deal?"

"You stay in contact with both me and Albert, via email and Skype, and I'll keep working on getting you an immunity deal. I understand that you need some time for yourself right now, but you're his family. He needs you."

I cocked my head to the side. "But I'm not his only family. Am I?" After leaving Brad and Albert to go after my father, I found myself returning over and over again to Albert leaning into Brad for comfort after I told him about Alexandra. My mind replayed the conversations they had, the looks they gave each other, the *old mans* and *sons* they exchanged. When I'd asked about their relationship, Brad had said *Albert is like a Father to me.* I'd never understood how Albert and his son Gregory could be estranged, but looking at Brad, I thought I knew why.

Brad's jaw dropped for a second, but then he recovered himself. "Albert tried to tell you."

"Evidently, not hard enough."

"I'm really sorry."

Part of me thought I should be mad about the secret they'd kept, but after all my secrets, I couldn't muster more than mild irritation at the deceit because I understood Albert's reasoning far too well. As Albert's son, Brad could have been used as leverage against him. It wasn't knowledge he wanted shared with Perun. "Don't be. I'm glad he's had you all these years. I'm glad he has you now. So what? He had an affair?"

Brad grimaced. "Albert? Good God, no. His wife had died. My mother had lost her husband. They used each other to lessen the pain."

"But Gregory found out and couldn't forgive him."

"Yes, but neither Albert nor Gregory even knew about me. My mom was restationed, and kept Albert in the dark about her pregnancy. I didn't meet Albert until after my mom died."

"I'm sorry."

Brad smiled. "Don't be. It is what it is. So do we have a deal? You'll stay in contact and email Albert at least a couple of times a week?"

"I was already planning to do that."

"Then it should be easy to promise."

"Jeez. Cross my heart and hope to die, stick a needle in my eye."

Brad laughed. "You're not lying are you?"

"You don't trust me?" I asked, trying my best to squelch a Machiavellian smile.

Brad shook his head, the corners of his mouth quirking up. "You keep forgetting, I know you Milena." Brad pulled my hand from the bucket and wrapped it in a fresh towel, applying pressure. "Does it feel like there are any shards still embedded when I apply pressure?"

I shook my head.

Brad patted my hand dry, then fished in the first aid kit the bartender brought, grabbing some alcohol wipes, ointment and gauze. "This is going to hurt," he said, taking out an alcohol wipe.

"Okay."

Brad wiped down each of my cuts, his eyes darting between my hand and my face, checking to see if I was okay. "You don't mind pain much, do you?"

"Not really."

"Hmmm," he said, grabbing the antibiotic ointment and slathering it on.

"Hmmm?"

While Brad wrapped my hand, I waited for him to say something, maybe along the lines of you need to see a shrink, but no words came. Finished, he looked up and smiled, reaching a hand to my cheek. The smile was small. Barely there, really. Others might not have seen it, but I did. His fingers skimmed over my skin. Now that I'd cooled down, they were warm not cold. I wanted to lean into them but didn't. "I've been where you are, M. I understand it. The external pain is a vent for the internal, but you need to find another outlet. You need to embrace what you're feeling instead of shoving it aside and ignoring it."

"So now you're a shrink? When did you get that degree?"

"I speak from experience. My mother was all I had, and when she died, when I found out about Albert, I didn't handle it well. I tried to ignore all my feelings, but you can't ignore that kind of stuff. You either work through it or find some way to vent without dealing. Like you, I did it through pain. Some people use alcohol or drugs, but nothing works for very long. You've gone from a high-school-cheerleader-baby-spy waiting for activation to a big, badass spy who's killed people in order to protect both her country and her friends. I imagine you're going to have some issues to deal with."

"You think?" I said. My eyes blinked madly, trying to stave off tears as I remembered my father's fear at the realization he'd played his last spy game and lost. I wouldn't mourn Mistress. She really was nothing to me. My father had been more though, and he was right, killing him did mess with my head. For every terrible memory of Father, I had another good one. I loathed him for what he became but couldn't forget what he was—the man who had beamed at me whenever I danced, who had called me Little O. I had my *freedom*, I wouldn't have to look over my shoulder worried about my father's revenge, but it came at a price. I wasn't sure I'd ever be truly free, not with the weight of my past.

"I'm not your enemy."

"I know that."

"Do you?" Brad tapped me on the head. "I think your brain believes it but not your heart. It's over, M. Don't live scared."

*Don't live scared?* I signaled the bartender for another drink as I tried to think of some way to respond. Was I living scared? I didn't think I was but maybe?

"On the house," said the bartender, putting two glasses down for Brad and I. I threw mine back before Brad could protest. When Brad didn't immediately go to drink his, I tried to grab it but came up short.

Brad's face contorted when the alcohol hit his taste buds then throat. "Gin? Ugh, tastes like a pine forest."

"I like nature," I said, throwing a few bills on the table and standing. "It's time for me to board."

Brad pulled a phone from his pocket and handed it to me. "It's a sat phone. I don't know how remote you're going, but this will work anywhere. No excuses, M. Call me when you land."

"Thanks," I said, pocketing the phone. "How come you never get my name wrong? You've never messed up. Not once. Even I get it wrong sometimes and Albert … well, he's hopeless."

Brad laughed. "In all my years of surveillance I never thought of you as Lex. You've always been Milena to me, the strong little girl in the impossible situation. The girl who grew up to be the strong woman before me now." Brad's fingers brushed my cheek on their way to tucking a stray piece of hair behind my ear. I wanted to lean into his hand but didn't.

Not up for a big, awkward goodbye scene with hugs and *bon voyages*, I smiled and gave his arm a quick pat before trying to move around him. He slid to the side, blocking me. Chucking me under the chin, he brought my eyes to his. "Be careful with Varos. He's a good guy, but he's not totally okay."

"I know."

"Two people who need to heal aren't always the best

companions. Don't be afraid to leave him, if you need to." Brad held my gaze for a second longer … searching … finding … then he leaned in and planted a kiss on my forehead before stepping aside. "I'll miss you."

I darted around him, afraid he'd change his mind, and hurried toward my plane without comment. Brad had said his piece, and I would stay in touch as promised. Nothing more needed saying.

But the farther away I got—two feet, five, ten—the more I felt a pull to turn back.

When the pull became too much, I stopped and pondered my shoes, which were, like me, scuffed and scratched. Brad had probably already left. I hadn't said goodbye. I hadn't waved. What was I going to say anyway? *Thanks for caring? Take care of Albert?* We'd already been over this stuff. I shook my head and started off again. I made it three or four more steps. *Damn it.*

They weren't red and sparkly like Dorothy's, but I tapped my battered boots together three times and turned. There was a crowd of people behind me, and I didn't see Brad. *Stupid. Stupid. Stupid.*

I was turning to leave when I saw him. He stood exactly where we parted. He hadn't moved an inch. Not one.

He waved.

I smiled and did the same.

"I'll miss you," I hollered.

Brad nodded, smiling wide.

# THIRTY-FIVE

## *University of St. Andrews, Scotland*
## *Three Years Later*

SITTING ON A bench outside the Modern History building, I ran nervous fingers through my hair, straightening it after its battle with the wind on the walk over. I glanced at my watch. Five minutes. Class would be done in five minutes. I pulled a folded sheet of paper from my purse and flipped it open, rereading my words scrawled in the margins.

Although the words satisfied me with their honesty, I wondered if I was about to make a terrible mistake. It had been three years, and Grant had moved on. His Facebook and Instagram accounts told me so. There was his freshman year girlfriend Eva who loved football games, Joss Whedon shows, and long walks in the park and then Greta, the water polo player who, if her social media pics were anything to go by, loved beer, beer, and more beer. In addition to Eva and Greta, Grant had joined a fraternity—Sigma Chi and looked to be living a full frat boy life, that is until he stepped away for a year abroad.

Now Grant was three months into his year away and the photos of drunken keggers were nowhere to be found. There weren't even any pictures of nights out at local bars. Instead, his accounts were full of artful pictures of local architecture and moody photos of the misty moors. Grant had returned to his photography and his relationship status was single, same as mine.

Was it wrong of me to come and try to start something again when he'd put me behind him? Was I being selfish? Or was I simply giving us the chance he'd asked for, albeit, three years late?

I rolled my neck from side-to-side and stood. *Stay or go? Stay or go?* I slid my hand over my abdomen feeling the swell of a new bird, number twenty-one. Twenty-one birds for twenty-one years.

Students began filing out of the history building. They looked so normal. Some laughing and smiling, talking with friends, others speeding off to their next destination. Was I ready for this?

My heart and stomach fluttered as Grant emerged, then I noticed he was sandwiched between two girls, chatting happily. My stomach dipped, and I stepped backward into the bench. My legs folded so I found myself seated again. The trio veered to the left, putting them in my path.

I stared at Grant, my hands wringing the printout of his last email, willing him to notice me. I tried to call out but couldn't, my voice an unintelligible garble. Now that the moment was here, my words were gone. Only a few feet away, Grant closed his eyes and threw his head back, laughing heartily. The two girls giggled. I continued to watch. I was stone. Rooted in place. My chest was so tight I couldn't breathe. He was two feet past me. Five. Ten. I was freezing up inside. All I'd fought to gain in the last three years was withering.

I closed my eyes and heaved in a breath. "Grant," I exhaled, the word barely a whisper. He didn't turn. "Grant," I said, again finding more of my voice. He kept walking, slipping out of my grasp. I jerked to my feet. "Grant!"

He turned, his eyes searching for the speaker. They wandered past me then sped back, growing wide. "Le… Milena," he said, incredulous.

I nodded, smiling. My chest relaxing, I was able to sneak in a few greedy breaths.

Grant quickly pivoted to the girls he was with and made his excuses. One shot me the stink eye, but the other only smiled and waved her goodbye. A few seconds later Grant's eyes were back on me. They wandered from my face to my feet and then back again as if I was an apparition. When our eyes finally met, neither of us moved. We stared, unblinking, drinking each other in. Seeing each other. Reading each other. Understanding each other.

Grant reached out a hand and skimmed my cheek. We'd stood ten feet apart but now, somehow, he was only a few feet away … touching me. I leaned into his hand and he smiled tucking a lock of hair behind my ear. His fingers ignited an internal hum as my nerve endings fired to life. "You look good," he said, grinning bashfully.

Still feeling strangely uncoordinated, I shoved the piece of paper I held at him. The wind tried to grab the paper as I fumbled, but somehow I got it into Grant's hands. With a raised eyebrow, Grant unfolded the crumpled paper. "I answered your questions."

"I see that," he said, nodding toward the bench I'd been sitting on. When I didn't move, he grabbed my hand and led me over. God. His hand. In mine. It felt so normal. So right.

Still holding my hand, his thumb rubbing my scar just

like he'd always done, Grant scanned my answers. At one of them, a broad smile crossed his face. "You're working on a book?" he asked. "I thought you said that would never happen?"

Relaxing into him, into this exchange, I laughed. "I've learned to never say never."

Grant nodded as he folded the piece of paper. One crease. Then another. And another. His efforts were slow and meticulous until finally he tucked the neat little parcel into his pocket. Instead of looking at me, he gazed across the quad to the horizon. His face gave nothing away. It was placid. Peaceful. He seemed so relaxed and unperturbed by my sudden appearance, I wondered if he'd put me so far behind him, that my visit meant nothing.

Not knowing what to say or do, I waited. He'd speak again or walk away. Either way I'd have my answer. After a few minutes Grant pulled out his phone and tapped away on it. What was he doing? Checking email? Playing a game? In order to see, I would have had to lean over, something my pride wouldn't allow. Why had he ditched his friends if this was what he wanted? Why not keep walking? Why touch my cheek? Why smile? God damn it! Why?

My nerves frayed, I was seconds from retreat when Grant handed me his phone. I looked down to find a draft email. It was a reply to the last email I'd sent, ending our relationship. "I know you said you wouldn't check this email again but …" Grant shrugged, heat rising in his cheeks.

Dear Milena,

I'm at University of St. Andrews in Scotland for the next year, if you change your mind and want to give us a try.

## Grant

The message was short, sweet and to the point. It was also a message he'd never sent. The draft date was from when he'd first arrived in Scotland. "You never sent it," I said, returning the phone.

"I've thought about it. Every damn day."

"Oh," I said, a half-smile creeping onto my face.

"Where you been?"

"Here and there."

It had started to drizzle and Grant pulled off his glasses to wipe them dry. "You with anyone?"

"I was with my old handler, Varos, in Zanzibar for a while. Albert and I spent last summer in Peru and the summer before that in New Zealand. But I've spent a lot of time alone to be honest, wandering from place to place."

"Hmmm," said Grant, studying me.

"You know something?"

Grant laughed. "I know many things."

I reached forward and lifted his chin with the tips of my fingers. His eyes were a tropical blue. Gorgeous. The color of the ocean in Zanzibar. They were the kind of eyes you wanted to lose yourself in. "I've really missed you."

# THIRTY-SIX

### *Washington D.C.*
### *Three Years Later*

I DIPPED A spoon into my hot chocolate and ferreted out a marshmallow, popping it into my mouth. Yum. "You're still going to be up for your book tour next month, right?" asked my literary agent, Lucy, her phone voice chipper like always.

"I'll definitely be up for it. I can't wait," I said, nodding to Mark as he entered the café. He slid into a seat opposite me and pushed forward a manila envelope.

"And don't forget about the interview with *Girl's Life Magazine*."

I laughed. "I won't forget. This is a dream come true, and I'm not going to miss a thing. Hey, can I call you back in a little bit? My meeting just showed up."

"Sure. Talk later. I can't wait for this launch. You're going to take the world by storm. I just know it. Goodbye normal. Hello fame!"

"God, I hope not," I said, wincing. "I'm all about the normal."

Lucy laughed. "We'll see."

I tucked the phone into my purse then opened the envelope pulling out a packet of papers. For the last two years, I'd been working with the CIA as a consultant. Turns out Perun wasn't the only organization with the bright idea of using children as sleeper agents to infiltrate key positions in the US. Given my first-hand experience as a child sleeper, Brad was able to broker an immunity deal for me in exchange for my expertise on the matter. Against all the odds, he got me the deal he promised, and today my contract was up. "Everything's set?" I asked, handing Mark a cup of coffee.

"Your consulting contract with the CIA is complete. You're free." Mark nodded at the diamond ring on my finger. "Although it doesn't look like you'll be a free woman for too much longer."

I smiled, fiddling with my engagement ring. "I won't be giving up my freedom, only gaining a partner in crime."

Mark laughed. "Yeah, I can see that. Both of you are always up to no good. I heard your memoir is coming out soon."

I nodded. "Don't worry it's being sold as complete fiction not a memoir. No one's going to believe a cheerleading-secret-agent-super-spy ever existed."

"Super spy? I think you're having delusions of grandeur," said Mark, smirking. "I did catch you."

"And I did escape."

Mark rolled his eyes, as was the norm in our conversations. During my time with the CIA, Mark and I developed a friendly-ish working relationship, although I think he liked me more than he was letting on. "Touché," said Mark.

I shoved the papers back in the envelope and put them in my purse. "I'll have my lawyer take a look at these."

"You don't trust me? I'm hurt."

Now it was my turn to roll my eyes. From my purse, I

pulled out a copy of my book and handed it to Mark. "For your reading pleasure. I even signed it for you."

The smirk on Mark's face fell just a little bit as he opened the cover to read my inscription.

*To Mark,*

*For finally agreeing to a deal I could live with.*

*Milena*

Mark smiled, closing the cover. "You should thank Brad. It was his relentlessness that got it done."

I smiled mischievously, and Mark rolled his eyes again. "That's my cue to leave. I'll see you around."

"See ya at the wedding," I called, giving my stomach a pat.

Mark waved his hand as he walked away. "Yeah. Yeah. We'll be there."

I sipped my hot chocolate and smiled, my heart going pitter-patter. In only a month, I'd be getting married. I, Milena Rokva, was marrying the man of my dreams. I'd never thought such a thing was possible. I had a fiancé and a career I loved and very soon I'd officially be a part of a very real and very normal family. And after I signed the CIA's release documents, I'd be a free woman, my spy life firmly in the rearview mirror.

My phone rang breaking my reverie. "Hello?"

"M, I forgot the wine for dinner. Can you stop by the ABC store and get both a white and a red?" asked Albert.

"Sure. I'll grab it and be over in forty. I got my release

papers today."

"Brad told me! That's why tonight's going to be a partay!"

"I have some other news to share, but that can wait. See you soon," I said, hanging up and heading for my car.

Monoculus noticed my exit and started barking immediately. "Hello, buddy. Ready to go see Daddy and Grandpa?" Mono bl*inked his one eye at* me then licked my fa*ce. "I'll take that* as an enthusiastic yes," I said, scratching behind his ears.

After slogging through D.C. traffic, I pulled into the ABC store in Fair Valley forty-five minutes later. I was running late. Very late. Not knowing much about wines, I scanned the shelves looking for a couple of moderately expensive bottles. Tonight there was a lot to celebrate.

"That Pegasus Bay Riesling is really nice," said a voice behind me. I knew that voice and turned immediately.

"You're back in town," I said, smiling and accosting Grant with a hug.

"Dad and I have a golfing trip this weekend."

"So you two are getting along better?" I asked, stepping back and giving Grant the once over. He looked good. Really good.

"We're trying to. He wasn't thrilled I decided to become an environmental lawyer. Dad told me about your book deal. Very cool."

"I dedicated the book to you, **since you g**ave me the idea."

"You didn't?"

"I most certainly did," I replied, squeezing his arm. "You look amazing by the way. You been working out?"

Grant grabbed the bottle of white he'd recommended and handed it to me. "My girlfriend's a yoga teacher. She's been working on my flexibility."

"This would be your plus one for the wedding! What's her

name? What's she like? Tell me everything? Can you find me a red?"

Grant picked a merlot and handed it over then looked at his watch. "Um?"

My eyes went wide. "Shit. I'm already late for family dinner. Hold that thought. Call me and we'll grab coffee. I want to hear everything." Clutching the two wine bottles, I leaned in and kissed his cheek. "I've missed you. You're my very favorite ex-boyfriend."

Grant wrapped an arm around my waist. "I've missed you, too. You're my very favorite ex-girlfriend."

I stepped back and smiled, my stomach twinging. Instead of a *what might have been*, Grant and I had an *almost but not quite*. Our year in Scotland had been amazing, but we never quite recaptured our original chemistry. Scotland was the year I finally grew into myself. I'd been in a holding pattern before that as I wandered from place to place. Scotland was where I found myself, and where I realized Grant and I weren't a love story. The real me wasn't right for Grant. He wanted it to be. For a while, he pretended that it was, but eventually there were cracks in his façade, and he couldn't hide that it wasn't working. I thought about trying to change because I did love him. But in the end, I couldn't do it. I'd fought too hard not to embrace my identity, for better or worse. "We'll always have Scotland," I offered.

Grant smiled wistfully. "Yes, we will. I'll see you soon. I'm holding you to that coffee date." He leaned in and kissed my forehead. "Now go. You're late."

# THIRTY-SEVEN

WITH MONOCULUS RUNNING circles around my legs, I shuffled my way to the front door of the old farmhouse trying not to face plant. An Australian shepherd, he was a sheep dog through and through and would herd anything and everything. Martine must have seen me struggling through a window because she opened the door and let out Ork, who barked, his tone commanding. Mono immediately stopped herding me and ran over to Ork for a nuzzle. They may have had a ten-year age gap, but they were still the best of friends. I dug a biscuit out of my purse and handed it to Ork on the way inside. "How're you doing old boy?" I asked, giving his snout a kiss. Ork was well past the typical life expectancy of a Scottish Deerhound but was still hanging in there.

"He's good. Gran's been feeding him scraps," said Martine, winking. "How ya feeling?" she asked, looking me up and down.

"Pretty damn good, all things considered."

Martine grabbed the wine bottles. "Tonight is going to be so fun!" she sang, skipping into the dining room where her model girlfriend, Izzy, was setting the table. Izzy and I gave each other a wave. Although she was a new addition to Martine's dating lineup, I had a feeling Izzy would be around for a while.

Amélie stuck her head out from the kitchen. "Hey, M. I made your favorite tonight, cassoulet."

I walked over to give her a hug. "I knew something smelled amazing." Dating my grandfather for almost three years now, Amélie was a regular and welcome fixture in the kitchen. With Amélie around, I knew Albert wouldn't starve.

Amélie kissed both my cheeks in turn. "You need to tell your fiancé to stop taste testing though. He's getting in my way."

I glanced behind Amélie and saw said fiancé standing over a cooking pot with spoon in hand. As usual the sight of him made my heart gallop merrily. His green eyes were a tether, drawing me in and holding me captive. Captivated. Here was my match. The man that knew me to my very core.

I smiled, walking over. "Tsk. Tsk."

Brad smirked wickedly as he wrapped an arm around my waist and offered me a spoonful. I laughed, opening my mouth wide.

I groaned at the tasty goodness just as Amélie grabbed the spoon from Brad and flicked a dishtowel at us. We retreated, giggling like little kids.

When we were safely away from the stove, Amélie set to finishing the meal while Brad guided me to a corner for a kiss. "How was your day?" he whispered, his lips meeting mine, softly at first then with an eagerness that bordered on inappropriate for our current location. My mind said to pull back, but my heart and body said no freaking way, so I let myself melt into him. Into us.

It was Albert who broke us apart by biffing Brad on

the head with a rolled up magazine as he walked into the kitchen. "Get a room, son. Get a room."

Brad leaned his forehead into mine and sighed, one of his hands coming to rest on my stomach. He kissed my nose then pulled back, shooting a nasty look at his dad. Albert chuckled and winked in reply. Seeing the two of them now, I wondered how I'd never noticed their similarities. They shared so many expressions and had such similar personalities.

Albert unrolled the magazine he was holding and flipped to a page inside. "Look who just got a glowing review for *They Call Me Cassandra Stone*."

I blushed waving him off. As much as I loved writing and creating stories, I wasn't interested in garnering any fame. I don't know if it was my past as a spy, or if I just wasn't that kind of person, but I didn't like the idea of being noticed as I walked down the street or strangers knowing my name. I was publishing the book under a pseudonym, but there were book signings scheduled and media interviews. The mere thought made my skin crawl. I had a normal life now or as close as I could get with a CIA fiancé, and I wasn't going to give that up.

"Dinner's ready," said Amélie, waving us out of the kitchen. "Go sit down and I'll bring it in."

We found Martine and Izzy being all lovey-dovey at the dinner table, their hands entwined, their heads bowed together.

"Hormones," lamented Albert, shaking his head.

Carrying a water jug, Amélie pinched Albert's butt before sliding the jug onto the table. "Hormones," she said, pulling back and wrapping her arms around Albert to kiss him square on the mouth. "Thank God for hormones."

Amélie retreated into the kitchen as Albert turned bright

red. “Get a room, old man,” said Brad.

Everyone laughed except for Albert, but the humor of the situation eventually overcame his embarrassment and he joined in too. I loved seeing everyone so happy. I loved this moment of normalness. It wasn’t just Albert and me sitting down to eat any more. Before, we had been a family of two. A family built on both love and lies. Now the lies were revealed and our family had expanded. No longer worried about putting others in danger because I might relay intel on his emotional weak spots, Albert had publicly acknowledged Brad as his son and started to date. Although Albert was a little slow as far as *courting* went, I was pretty sure, Brad and I wouldn’t be having the only wedding this year.

I absently fingered the locket at my neck, sliding it on its chain. Instead of pictures of Alexandra’s parents, it now held a picture of Albert and my mother Sibel. I thought of the locket as mine now, well and truly. It signified my past as Alexandra Gastone, my present as Milena Rokva and my future as Milena Gastone. Despite a rocky start, life was good now. Not perfect, but good. I had baggage—Varos, my brothers in jail, my biological parents, the list was long. They were the darkness lurking on the periphery of my happiness, but I’d grown strong enough to keep them on the periphery and not let them drag me down. I had too much to be thankful for.

What I had might be a ragtag, cobbled together family, but they were mine and they were perfect.

Amélie brought in the cassoulet and Albert poured wine as Amélie doled out heaping platefuls to everyone. “Bon appétit.”

“I have a toast to make,” said Albert raising his glass. “To family,” he said, beaming at everyone in turn.

My heart melted just a little when he held Amélie’s gaze

the longest. Love was written all over his face. And all over hers. No, mine wouldn't be the only wedding this year.

"To family," we sang in unison.

"And speaking of ..." said Brad, reaching for my hand under the table and running a thumb over my little black bird. His glass was raised to the table, but his eyes were on me ...

Seeing me ...

Knowing me ...

Loving me ... Milena Rokva.

"That family will be expanding by one come September."

Thank you for reading *My Name is Milena Rokva*. Hope you enjoyed it!

Would you like to know when my next book will be released or keep up with my news? Visit my website at **TAMACLAGAN.COM** and sign up for my newsletter! I also love interacting with readers on Twitter and Facebook. Don't be shy!

# ACKNOWLEDGEMENTS

Much gratitude goes to my agent, Lucy Carson, for telling me to go for it and self-publish the sequel to Alexandra Gastone when my publisher closed. You rock!

And, as always, many thanks to my beta readers Carol Rinne, Marissa Kennerson, Pintip Dunn, and Madeline Dyer. Special thanks to Paula Stokes for her wonderful editorial critique. You rocked it!

Much appreciation goes to my YA Story Sisters for their love and support in this writing journey. You ladies are amazing!

And finally, a huge hug and thanks to my family—Mom, Dad, David, Zac, Margaret and Robert—love you lots and thank you, thank you, thank you for being so supportive!

A special thanks to all those who helped spread the word via Facebook about the Alexandra Gastone release last year. My sincerest apologies if I've missed anyone. If your profile was set to private, I may not have seen that you shared about the release.

Shannon Gardner Stockton
Phyllis Jeffreys Culbreth
Abby Maurin Spell
Terri Gillispie Walling
Kristin Elliott
Rachel Rowlands

Julie Nunweek
Melissa Brown Muckart
Robert Garnett
Allison Foley
Kelly Newell Eisenbraun
Janet Hart
Liz Kinast
William de Wyke
Rebecca Ward
Michelle O'Connor Rieb
Kristi Marissa Alfaro
Amanda Fischer
Christian Taylor
Lana Simpson
Stephanie Fox Smithwick
Christina Brown Phillips
Mary Lynn Nesbitt Crawford
Garrett Smith
Molly Smith
Alonso Cordoba
Martha Maurin
Andrew Jack
Meredith Goodrum Connell
Andrea Lindsay Washo
Fran Wilson
Jo Drysdall
David Maclagan
Shannon Gamber
Sarah Hulcher
Lauren Palmer
Meredith Welch-Devine
Jason Atkinson
Jewel Rinne

Carmel La
Rebecca Butler Patrick
Will Howard
Sam Reading Nook NZ
Heather Brown Moore

# ABOUT THE AUTHOR

T.A. MACLAGAN is a Kansas girl by birth but has lived all over the world, including ten years in New Zealand. With a bachelor's degree in biology and a Ph.D. in anthropology, she's studied poison dart frogs in the rainforests of Costa Rica, howler monkeys in Panama, and the very exotic and always elusive American farmer. It was as she was writing her "just the facts" dissertation that T.A. felt the call to pursue something more imaginative and discovered a passion for creative writing. They Call Me Alexandra Gastone is her first novel.

Visit T.A. Maclagan on her website:

**TAMACLAGAN.COM**

Made in the USA
Monee, IL
14 August 2020

38471161R00152